판문점

바이링궐 에디션 한국 현대 소설 026

Bi-lingual Edition Modern Korean Literature 026

Panmunjom

이호철
판문점

Yi Ho-chol

ASIA
PUBLISHERS

Contents

판문점

Panmunjom

새벽녘에는 빗방울이 들었으나 어느새 구름으로 꽉 덮였던 하늘의 이 구석 저 구석이 뚫리며 비도 멎고 스름스름 개기 시작했다. 그렇다고 쨍하게 맑은 날씨로 활짝 개어 오른 것은 아니고 적당히 구름이 끼고 바람이 불며 꾸물거리는 변덕스러운 날씨로 변했다. 해가 떠오르자 비 갠 끝의 습기를 바람이 몰아가고 거무튀튀한 떼구름이 온 하늘을 와당탕 소리를 내듯 이리저리 몰려다녔다. 햇덩이는 그 희고 짙은 모습을 잠시 나타냈다가는 검은 구름 속에 묻혀 눈이 시지 않고도 바라볼 수 있게 귀여운 모습의 또렷한 윤곽이 되기도 하고, 육중한 떼구름에 휩싸여 빠져나오려고 안간힘을 쓰기도 했다. 함석지붕들이 새말갛

Raindrops began pattering on the ground at dawn. It was not long, though, before the rain stopped, holes appearing in the thick cloud cover. But this didn't mean a bright, clear day was in the offing. The sky remained peppered with storm clouds, and the wind continued to blow—it was fickle, capricious weather. As the sun rose, the wind swirled up, chasing away the fresh, moist air that follows the rain. Dark, gloomy patches raced from one end of the sky to the other. The sun burst out in a white glow only to be covered again in a murky pool of blackness; it would then etch itself in the sky, revealing to the naked eye the full glory of its pre-

게 반짝이는가 하면 어느새 그늘에 덮여 둔탁해지기도 하였다. 볕과 그늘이 뒤바뀌고 게다가 바람까지 불어, 거리는 수선스럽게 들떠 보였다.

정각 여덟 시에 버스는 조선 호텔 앞을 떠났다. 금방 서울을 빠져나오자 추수가 끝난 황량한 들판을 마른 먼지를 일으키며 내처 달렸다.

진수(鎭守)는 초행길이었다.

"내일 판문점 구경 가게 됐어요."

하고 어제 초저녁 형님에게 말하자,

"뭐, 판문점? 글쎄, 가는 것은 좋다만 조심해라."

형님은 이렇게 긴치 않게 받았다.

"을씨년스럽지 무슨 구경이 되겠어요. 끔찍스러."

하고 급하게 웃저고리를 걸치고 난 형수가 형님을 흘끗 쳐다보며 한마디 했다.

웃저고리를 갈아입은 형수에게서는 방 전체에 떠도는 화장품 냄새와 더불어 약간 야한 냄새가 났다. 필요 이상으로 도사연해서 앉아 있는 형님에게서도 비슷하게 역겨운 것이 풍겼다.

"끔찍스럽긴 무엇이 끔찍스러워."

형님이 형수를 향해 괜히 눈을 부릅뜬다.

cious circular outline as it tried valiantly to break free once more from the heavy bank of clouds enveloping it. Galvanized iron roofs brightly shimmered for an instant only to fade quickly into dullness. Sun turned to shade, shade back to sun, as the wind swept through the streets, packing them with a sense of disorder and excitement.

The bus left the Chosun Hotel at eight o'clock sharp. It had passed through Seoul in no time and was hurtling through the desolate fields emptied by the harvest, leaving a trail of dry dust in its wake.

This was the first time for Jinsu.

"I'm going to Panmunjom tomorrow," Jinsu had informed his older brother early the previous evening.

"What? Panmunjom? Well, nothing wrong with going there, I guess. But be careful," Older Brother had warned nonchalantly.

Jinsu's sister-in-law was hastily putting on her blouse. "What a god-awful place! What's there to see at a place like that? Gives me the creeps," she said, casting her husband a quick glance.

Sister-in-Law who had just changed her blouse gave off a rather wanton smell mixed with the scent of her make-up that was floating around the entire

'옳지, 저렇게 위엄을 부리는구나. 좀 전에 굉장히 사랑을 했는가 보군. 괜히 쓰윽, 내가 있으니까.'

진수는 마음속으로 이렇게 웃었다. 형수는 한순간 약간 풀이 죽은 낯색이 되었다가 곧 되살아났다.

"무슨 별 준빈 없어두 되나?"

형님 들으라는 말이 분명하여 진수는 형님이 대답하거니 알고 그편을 바라보았다.

그러나 형님은 석간을 들여다보면서 형수 말을 묵살하였다.

그제야 진수가 다급하게 대답하였다.

"무슨 준비가 필요해요, 필요 없어요."

형님은 다시 온전하게 따스한 낯색이지만 근친다운 우려도 약간 깃들인 투로 말하였다.

"하여튼 조심해라."

"네."

더블베드에 누일 법도 한데 더블베드는 비어 있고 조카아이는 바닥에 눕혔다. 라디오에서는 가느다란 음악이 흘러나왔다. 형수가 그것을 껐다. 형수의 조심스럽게 핥는 듯한 눈길이 잠시 형님의 몸 둘레를 감돌았다. 형님은 턱수염을 만지작거리면서 그냥 신문만 들여다보았다. 다시

room. Older Brother was sitting upright in an overly dignified manner, even as he himself exuded a nauseating, pungent smell.

"The creeps? Just what is it that gives you the creeps?" Older Brother gave his wife a needlessly stern, reprimanding glare.

Sure, put on a stately air. Must have really gone at it in bed just a moment ago. And now acting like this. Just because I'm here.

Jinsu laughed to himself.

Sister-in-Law was crestfallen for a moment but soon recovered her spirits. "Is there anything in particular I should prepare for your trip?"

This question was obviously for the benefit of Older Brother, and so it was in his direction that Jinsu glanced in anticipation of a response.

But Older Brother ignored his wife, absorbing himself in the evening paper.

"There's no need to get anything ready, no need at all," Jinsu put in quickly.

"In any event, be careful," repeated Older Brother in a perfectly genial tone, one tinged ever so slightly with the proper amount of concern to be shown for a family member.

"I will."

형수는 진수를 건너다보며 조금 미안한 얼굴을 하였다.
형님을 바라보다가 진수에게로 돌리는 그 표정의 변화가
엄청나게 느껴졌다.

"몇 시간이나 걸려요?"

형수가 또 물었다.

"한 두어 시간 걸린다더군요."

"아이, 좀 지루하겠군."

하고 형님 쪽을 또 쳐다보면서 하는 형수의 말은 '안 그렇
소, 여보' 하고 형님의 얼굴을 이쪽으로 돌려 잡자는 속셈
같았다.

형님은 일부러 그러는 것이 완연하게 그냥저냥 신문에
만 두 눈을 꼬나 박고 있었다.

마침 조카아이가 깨어 칭얼거렸다. 형수가,

"응, 응, 잘 잤니, 푸욱 잤어? 어이쿠, 기지개를 다 켜구,
어이쿠, 됐다아."

'이것 좀 봐요. 여보, 애 기지개 켜는 것 좀 봐요. 좀 보
래두.'

이렇게 또 형수는 형님을 쳐다보다가 제 김에 조금 뾰
로통해지는 듯했으나, 진수 편을 힐끗 보고는 다시 차악
가라앉아졌다.

Jinsu's nephew was lying asleep on the floor—he normally slept on the double bed. The radio was playing low, soft music. Sister-in-Law turned it off. She gave her husband a careful, embracing look and then turned away. Older Brother ran his fingers through his beard, engrossed in his newspaper. Sister-in-Law glanced over, somewhat apologetically, at Jinsu. It was remarkable, the difference between this look and the one she had just given her husband.

"How long does it take to get there?" she asked.

"A couple of hours supposedly."

"That long? Sounds pretty tedious," she said, looking over at her husband as if to say, *Isn't that right, dear?* She was less interested in discussing the particulars of the trip than in trying to get her husband to look up at her.

Older Brother seemed to go out of his way to keep his eyes fixed on his paper.

The baby woke up and started whimpering.

"There, there, did you have a nice little nap? Did you? Oh, he's stretching himself out. So cute." Sister-in-Law glanced at her husband again, as if to say, *Take a look at this. Look at the baby stretching his arms and legs, dear. Look.* It seemed for a moment

젖을 물렸다.

문득 형수는 진수를 향해 두 눈을 끔쩍끔쩍하고는 다시 애를 들여다보며 물었다.

"종혁아, 아재 어딨니?"

진수는 별 뜻도 없이 히죽 웃었다.

조카아이는 젖을 문 채 한 팔을 뒤로 돌리며 진수 편을 가리켰다.

"응, 거깄어?"

"또 아빠는?"

조카는 다시 같은 몸놀림으로 형님 쪽을 가리켰다.

"응, 아빠는 거기 있군."

하고 형수는 통째로 깨물어 먹고 싶은 듯이 와락 조카를 끌어안았다.

비로소 형님이 눈길을 들었다. 순간 형수의 눈빛이 반짝 했으나 형이 형수나 조카는 거들떠보지도 않는 것을 알자 다소곳이 머리를 수그리며 조심스럽게 애를 들여다보았다.

"몇 시에 떠나니?"

형님이 진수를 향해 조금 단호한 억양으로 물었다.

"여덟 시에 조선 호텔 앞에서 떠나요."

as if she was going to start sulking, but then she caught sight of Jinsu out of the corner of her eye and quickly recovered her composure. She began to breast-feed the baby.

Suddenly she jerked her head toward Jinsu, gave him a wink, and then looked back down at her baby.

"Where's your uncle, Jong-hyeok?" she asked.

A smile crept across Jinsu's face.

The baby, still sucking at his mother's breast, lifted up his arm and pointed at Jinsu.

"Oh, is that where he is? And how about Daddy?"

The baby pointed at Older Brother.

"Oh, that's where Daddy is," Sister-in-Law cooed, hugging her baby tightly as if she were going to swallow him whole.

Older Brother raised his head for the first time. Sister-in-Law's eyes flickered with hope, but when she saw that he was taking no notice whatsoever of what she was doing, she gently lowered her gaze toward her baby.

"What time are you leaving?" Older Brother asked somewhat stiffly.

"We leave from the Chosun Hotel at eight o'clock."

17

이젠 나가라는 신호인 듯해서 진수는 부스스 일어서 형님 방을 나왔다. 그리고 생각했다.

자기가 나왔으니까 형님과 조카의 사이는 온전하게 그들대로의 분위기로 돌아갔을 것이다. 형님은 와락 다가앉으며 형수의 엉덩이를 한번 꼬집어 볼 수도 있을 것이다. "아이, 왜 이래요오. 주책없이." 형수는 이렇게 소곤대는 목소리로 눈을 흘길 것이다. "안방에서 들어요. 이러지 말아요. 글세, 주책없이." 그러나 형수도 알고 있을 것이다. 그들만의 자리가 됐으니까 이러는 것을. 으레 딴 사람이 있으면 사또님이나 된 것처럼 근엄하게 도사리고 있는 남편을. 자연스럽고도 능청맞게 오므라졌다, 퍼졌다 하는 남편의 그 융통성에 속으로는 감탄할는지도 모른다. 정작 그들만의 분위기가 되면 형님은 애송이처럼 응석을 부리고 도리어 형수가 조금 전의 형님 같은 표정이 될지도 모른다. 형님이 애걸조가 되고 형수가 비싸게 굴지도 모른다. 여자란 은근히 이런 것을 바라고 있을지도 모른다. 사실 형님에겐 치사한 구석이 있다. 형수와 조카는 끔찍이 사랑하고, 어머니나 자기를 두고는 집안에서의 제 처신, 마땅히 해야 할 제 도리 같은 것만 우선 생각한다. 그리고 그 처신이나 도리는 적당히 작위적인 진지성을 수반하기

This question seemed to be the signal for him to go. Jinsu got up and quietly left the room.

No doubt all of them—Older Brother, Sister-in-Law, the baby—would reenter their own world now that he was gone. Nothing would stop Older Brother now from sliding over to Sister-in-Law and giving her a pinch on the behind. "Hey, what do you think you're doing? Where are your manners?" Sister-in-Law would whisper, giving him a dirty look. "They'll hear us in the other room. Stop it. Don't you have any shame?"

But Sister-in-Law would understand. Her husband was acting like this because the three of them were alone—the same man who put on the dignified air of an esteemed official if someone else happened to be present. No doubt she would marvel to herself at the naturalness, and the two-facedness, with which her husband was able to alter his demeanor. It was entirely possible that once they were alone the roles would be reversed. Older Brother would play the baby, begging for attention, while Sister-in-Law would assume a stately, detached air. Older Brother would speak in pleading tones as Sister-in-Law severely reprimanded him. That was probably what women secretly wanted. The fact of the matter was

가 일쑤이다.

'어머님이 원래 동태찌개를 좋아하시는데, 저녁엔 그것 좀 하지 그랬어. 그러구 어머님이 늙으시구 쓸쓸하시어서 이것저것 잔소리가 심할 테지만 그런 걸 고깝게 여기면 못쓰니까 조심하구, 겸상으로 밥을 먹을 때도 진수는 내 밥그릇과 제 밥그릇을 은근히 살피고 있어. 그런 건 아무리 소탈한 사람이라도 미묘하게 작용하는 법이니까 당신이 자상히 신경을 써야 돼. 진국(鎭國)이한테서 어제 기별이 온 모양인데, 돈을 좀 부쳐 달라는가 봐. I need money. 마지막에 조심스럽게 이렇게 썼더라잖아. 진수 얘긴 농담 비슷했지만 아무래도 좀 부쳐 줘야 할까 봐. 지금 얼마 남아 있어? 그쪽 돈은 말구, 종혁이 이름으로 된 통장 있잖아. 거기서 좀 떼보지그래.' 설령 그들만이 됐을 때 이렇게 제 아내에게 차근차근 말을 한다 해도 그러는 표정에는 작위적인 것이 번뜩일 것이다. 비록 형수가 이런 설교를 들으며 순순히 받아들이는 표정이었다고 하더라도, 조금만 지나면 그런 것은 아무래도 좋고 까마득히 잊어버릴 것이다. 형님은 더욱 치근덕거리며 형수에게로 다가앉을지도 모른다. 이렇게 한집에서조차 느껴지는 이

that there was something disgraceful in Older Brother's behavior. He was unsparing in the love he gave to his wife and baby. But when his thoughts turned to his mother and Jinsu, all he cared about was his own position in the household. The only thing that concerned him was how to do what was expected of him, how to properly perform his role as the eldest son. What was more, he always managed to play this role to a T, displaying just the right amount of sincerity.

"Mother likes pollack stew—you should have made it for dinner. And Mother is getting on in years, she's lonely. She's bound to start nagging more and more. So be understanding. Don't take it the wrong way. Jinsu seems to be comparing the food on his plate to mine when we all sit down and eat together. Even though he's not a stickler about things like that, it's bound to get to him sooner or later, so make sure you do something about it. Jinsu got a message from Jinguk yesterday. Seems he's asking us to send money. According to Jinsu, he wrote 'I need money' out neatly in English at the bottom of the letter. Jinsu said it as if it were a joke, but we should probably send something anyway. How much do we have? Not *that* money. How

역감, 일정한 상거가 이즈음 와서 진수로 하여금 구체적으로 여자라는 것, 결혼이라는 것을 생각하게 하는 것이다. 그러나 좀 전에 형님이 "가는 것도 좋지만 조심해라" 하던 그 근친다운 우려의 눈길은 진수로서 그러지 않아도 외포가 곁들인 판문점행을 더욱 꺼림칙하게 한 것만은 틀림이 없었다. 간밤 내내 판문점이라는 곳이 풍겨 주는 이 역감은 니깃니깃한 기름기로서 소용돌이쳤다. 판문점이 중유 같은 물큰물큰한 액체 더미가 되어 우르르 자갈 소리를 내면서 몰려오기도 하고, 우둘투둘한 바윗덩어리로서 우당탕거리며 달아나기도 했다. 그런가 하면 판문점이 상투를 한 험상궂은 노인이기도 했다. 시뻘건 두루마기를 입고 가로 버티고 서서 이놈 소리를 지르기도 했다. 호되게 매를 맞은 일이 있는 국민학교 4학년 때 담임선생이기도 했다. 밤새 판문점에서 쫓겨다니는 꿈을 꾸었다.

새벽에 집을 나서는데 어머니가 말했다.

"조심해라, 또 덤벙대지 말구."

"네."

어머니의 그 자애로운 눈길을 쳐다보며 진수는 '어머니가 역시 제일 좋군. 혼자 늙어지면 참 삭막할 거라' 하고 조금 쓸쓸한 생각을 했다.

about the account in Jong-hyeok's name? Take some out of that."

Even if Older Brother went through all these details with his wife when they were alone, the expression on his face would betray a certain forcedness, an artificiality. And even if Sister-in-Law listened quietly to his sermonizing, seemingly taking it all in, it would not be long before she would forget about it, thinking it would be all right to let things go. Maybe Older Brother would slide over to Sister-in-Law with more on his mind than just pinching her.

This sense of estrangement, this distance that could be felt even between family members living under the same roof, had lately been making Jinsu think more concretely about what a woman was, what marriage meant.

At the same time, it could not be denied that Older Brother's display of concern, his saying, "Well, nothing wrong with going there, I guess. But be careful," did have the effect of making Jinsu feel even more uneasy about the impending trip to Panmunjom.

Panmunjom swirled around him all night like a thick coat of oil, pouring itself over him, separating

한 시간 남짓 달린 버스 속은 외국인 기자들의 웃음소리와 잡담으로 하여 또 다른 이역의 분위기로 무르익어 있었다. 그것은 집에서처럼 섬세하게 느껴지는 미묘한 이역감이 아니라 뚜렷한 이역감이었다.

서양 사람들이란 한 사람 한 사람 따로따로 보면 별로 구별이 없는 듯하지만, 몇 사람을 한데 놓고 차근차근 뜯어보면 제각기의 특색을 특색대로 찾아낼 수가 있다.

대개 머리통이 크고 머리칼은 샛노랗기도 하고 짙은 다갈색이기도 하고, 그런가 하면 신비스럽도록 보얀 은실빛이기도 하고 눈알 빛 또한 가지각색이다. 꼭 장난질로 물감 칠을 한 유리알을 박아 놓은 듯이 영롱하게 새파란 눈, 보랏빛 눈, 혹은 회색빛이 도는 눈, 게다가 육중한 코, 전체로서 꽤나 입체적으로 음영이 짙으면서도 어느 구석인가 잔뜩 입김을 불어넣어서 풍선처럼 부풀게 한 것 같은 멀렁한 얼굴, 팔, 다리, 손등 할 것 없이 부성부성하게 노르께한 솜털…… 도무지 사람 같지가 않고 괴이한 짐승처럼 보이는 것이다. 그러나 표정 하나하나의 움직임과 노는 짓들은 순진성과 간교성을 범벅으로 지니고 있고, 우리네보다 훨씬 낙천적인 구석이 있어 보인다. 그리고 그 노는 짓들을 가만히 살펴보면 제각기 그 성격의 윤곽들도

him from all that surrounded him, alienating him. The oil seemed to grow thicker and thicker, a viscous mass roaring over him. But then it transformed itself into a boulder crashing off into the distance. Now it was a stern, fearsome old man with a top-knot, dressed in a crimson overcoat, towering over Jinsu, screaming at him, "You bastard." Suddenly Panmunjom became his fourth-grade homeroom teacher, the one who had once whipped him so severely. Panmunjom chased him through his dreams the entire night.

"Be careful. Don't do anything foolish," Jinsu's mother said as he was leaving the house early in the morning.

"Don't worry."

Jinsu was overcome by a certain sorrow as he looked into his mother's loving eyes. *You're the best, Mother. How sad it must be to grow old all by yourself.*

A little over an hour had passed since their departure from the Chosun Hotel. The banter of foreign reporters filled the bus, making Jinsu feel very much on the outside of things. This feeling, however, was clear, vivid, not at all resembling the subtle sense of alienation he had felt at home.

금방 짚이는 것이다. 맨 앞쪽에 몸을 쉴 사이 없이 움직이며 웃음거리나 없나 해서 잔뜩 기갈이 들린 좀 주책없어 보이는 사람, 원체 앞자리가 멀어서 말은 못 알아듣겠지만 그 과장이 섞인 손놀림과 요란스러운 뒷모습, 얘기를 듣는 사람들의 심드렁한 표정 등으로 미루어 별로 우습지도 않은 얘기를 애써 우습게 얘기하려는 것이 완연하였다. 한 대목이 끝나면 이따금 그 주위에서 한가한 웃음이 터지곤 하지만 어쩐지 보기에도 딱했다. 정말 우스운 것이라면 이 정도로 떨어진 자리에서도 그 분위기에 저도 모르게 전염되어 웃음이 비어져 나올 것이다. 그러나 이따금 터지는 그쪽의 한가한 웃음은 이 버스 칸 전체의 메마름을 차라리 의식하게 해주고, 그럴수록 진수에겐 생소한 이역감만을 배가시키는 것이다. 더더구나 그 작자 바로 앞에 앉은 사람은 자못 호인풍이어서, 그 작자에게서 좀 놓여나고 싶은 모양이지만, 할 수 없이 억지로 꾹 참고 견디는 얼굴이 이쪽에서 보는 사람조차 슬그머니 조바심이 나고 안타까워졌다. 드디어는 하품이 나오자 힐끗 그 앞사람 표정을 살피고는 반쯤 입을 벌리는 듯하다가 어물어물 다시 다물어 버린다. 순간 그 작자도 잠시 그쳤다가 염치없이 다시 얘기를 잇는다.

Viewed apart, one by one, there's not much to dis-
tinguish one Westerner from another. But if you put
them in a group and look long and hard, the differ-
ences in their features gradually become apparent.

Their heads are usually large, their hair blond or
dark brown, their skin an almost mystifying silvery
white. Their eyes come in all colors, light blue, indigo, gray—brilliantly colored toy glass beads seem to
have been placed in their eye sockets. Their noses
are rather large. While they generally have clear-cut,
angular features, something about their faces lends
them a certain balloonlike puffiness. A thick yellow
peach fuzz covers their hands, arms, legs. It's almost
as if they're not quite human, something out of this
world. Their body movements, their facial expressions, give off an air that can best be described as a
mix of naiveté and cunning. At the same time, they
certainly do seem more positive, optimistic than we
are. If you look carefully at individual body lan-
guage, you can get a very good feel for the overall
personality of each one of them.

The one at the very front of the bus making all
sorts of gestures as if he was dying to find something funny to say seemed to be on the light-headed
side. He was sitting far away, so there was no way

진수는 뒤쪽에 앉아 혼자 히죽이 웃었다. 순간 공교롭게도 그자와 눈이 마주쳤다. 그도 조금 창피한 듯 히죽 웃고는 외면을 하고 있었다.

　'사람들이란 참 묘해. 이렇게 멀리 앉아 있어도 어떤 순간, 한눈에 완벽한 교류가 가능해지니 말야.'

　바로 그때 진수 뒤에서 우렁우렁한 목소리가 울렸다. 물론 영어였다.

　"헤이, 캐나리, 무얼 그리 또 짖어대구 있어?"

　'아이쿠, 시원해라. 나 말구두 또 있었구먼.'

　진수는 번쩍 정신이 들듯이 뒤를 돌아보았다.

　버스 속이 술렁대었다.

　"뭐라구?"

　앞쪽 당사자가 휘딱 돌아보며 받았다.

　"보아하니, 그닥 재미가 없는 얘기 같은데, 대관절 무슨 얘길 혼자서만 신바람이 나서 그 야단이야? 보고 있자니 딴 사람들이 딱하지 않나. 난 미리 피해서 여기 와 앉았지만."

　'어이쿠, 시원해라. 저런 것이 사람을 죽이지, 죽여. 그자도 기가 꺾일 걸.'

　순간 온 버스 칸이 들썩이도록 웃음이 터졌다. 누구나

to hear what he was saying. But judging from his loud, exaggerated gesticulations, as well as from the glum expressions of his listeners, it was obvious that he was trying too hard to make a funny story out of something that wasn't the least bit amusing. He'd pause every once in a while and occasionally get a few empty laughs. It was pathetic to watch. If what he was saying was genuinely funny, the whole bus would have been hooting and hollering, even the people sitting in the back.

The occasional empty laughter from the front only served to cast an even deeper gloom over the bus, heightening the already keen sense of estrangement Jinsu was feeling. The fact that the person sitting right across from this guy seemed like an altogether sensible, likable fellow, one who clearly wanted to somehow get away from him but was forced to sit there and take it, made Jinsu, even though he was sitting all the way in the back, feel even more anxious and distressed. Finally, this man yawned and gave the guy a look. He opened his mouth as if he was about to say something, but then stopped himself. The storyteller paused briefly, but then went on without paying him further attention.

A smile flickered across Jinsu's face. At that

가 그 작자가 빚어내는 버스 안의 탁한 분위기를 똑같이 역겹게 느끼고 있었던 모양이었다.

"오키나와 얘기야."

그 작자가 받았다.

"오키나와가 어쨌기?"

뒷사람이 다시 질러댔다.

"오키나와 풍속 얘기."

이번엔 그 작자 앞의, 조금 전에 하품을 하던 자가 받았다.

"다 아는 얘길 뭘 지껄여."

"오키나와 여잔 맨발로 다닌대나."

"별 신통한 얘기도 아니군그래."

맨 뒷자리에 앉았던 또 다른 녀석 하나가 이렇게 가시 돋친 소리로 톡 쏘았다.

순간 버스 안은 다시 조용해졌다. 모두가 어느 맨바닥으로 풀썩 주저앉은 표정으로 제각기 손목시계들을 보았다. 새삼스럽게 버스 엔진 소리가 와랑와랑 부풀어 오르고 누구인가가 한국말로, "아직 멀었나?" 하고 지껄이고 있었다.

문득 진수의 눈엔 건너편 자리에서 투박한 남색 코트

moment, his eyes met those of the man who had just yawned. The man smiled in return, as if he was a little embarrassed, and then looked away.

That's the uncanny thing about people. No matter how much distance separates you, your eyes meet for an instant and you're able to come to a complete understanding.

Suddenly a voice boomed out from behind Jinsu. In English, of course. "Hey, Connolly, just what is it you're making such a big deal about?"

What a relief! Someone else who feels the same way. Jinsu felt something of a surge inside and turned around quickly. There was a little commotion among the passengers.

"What?" asked the storyteller, jerking his head toward the back of the bus.

"Doesn't seem like anyone much cares about what you've got to say. So why are you getting so worked up? Doesn't look like anyone wants to hear it. I'm sitting way back here just to get away from you."

Whew! That's enough to cut anyone down to size. That should shut him up.

The whole bus burst out into laughter. It seemed that this guy had been grating on everyone's nerves.

차림인 늙수그레한 여기자 하나가 주위의 이런 동정에는 아랑곳없이 소곤소곤 열심히 재잘거리고 있는 것이 돋보였다. 그 옆의 남자는 남편이라는 것이어서 부부 동반으로 나와 있는 기자들이라는 것이다. 그러고 보니까 역시 말하는 표정에 집안 얘기다운 자상하고도 따뜻한 구석이 느껴진다. 남편은 홈스펀 웃저고리에 코르덴 바지의 수수한 차림이고 두툼한 고불통을 물었지만 아무리 보아도 들이빠는 기척이 없다. 이제나저제나 하고 안타깝게 바라보는 것이나 전혀 들이빨지는 않는다. 저런 망할 자식이, 드디어 진수는 이렇게 악을 쓰듯이 속을 뇌까렸다. 아내 쪽은 보지 않고 똑바로 제 앞만 바라보고 있는 것이 엊저녁의 형님처럼 그런대로 남편다운 위엄이 늠름하다. 한참만에야 드디어 뻑뻑 힘을 주어 고불통을 빨다가 얌전한 손놀림으로 고불통 끝을 만져 보고, 불이 꺼진 것을 알아차리고도 전혀 표정이 없이 호주머니에서 라이터를 꺼내 불을 댕겼다. 잠시 말을 끊고 이러는 남편을 아내가 차근히 지켜본다. 둘 사이의 더께가 앉을 정도의 때문은 익숙함이 단려하게 느껴진다. 그러나 그 단려한 냄새도 역시 어딘가 서양풍의 이역 냄새였다. 둘이 다 팔자 좋게 곱게 걸어온 그들 인생의 편린이 번뜩였다. 드디어 남편의 담

"It's about Okinawa," he said.

"What about it?" asked the man in back.

"I was just describing some of the customs over there."

"Stuff everyone already knows about," added the man in front who had yawned a moment before.

"I was talking about how Okinawan women go around in their bare feet."

"Now there's something to remember," shot another reporter derisively from the very back.

The bus suddenly fell quiet again. All seemed to sink despondently into their seats; a number of people looked down heavily at their watches. The roar of the engine sounded louder. "How much farther is it?" asked someone in Korean.

An older woman reporter across the way dressed in a coarse indigo coat suddenly caught Jinsu's eye. She was speaking in low tones, oblivious to anything happening on the bus. Her husband was next to her—the two of them must have been sent out on assignment together. The look on her face was warm and affectionate, the kind of expression one gets when talking about family matters. Her husband was dressed neatly but plainly in corduroy pants and a tweed jacket. A large pipe dangled from

33

뱃불이 댕겨지고 푸른 연기가 고불통에서 피어나자, 아내의 얼굴에도 비로소 안심하는 표정이 떠오른다. 다시 좀 전의 얘기를 계속한다.

하버드(대학)에 다니는 큰아이는 위가 약해서 탈이야요. 어제 편지에도 그저 위 타령이군요. 참, 내 정신 좀 봐, 깜박 잊었었네. 후리맨한테서도 편지가 왔어요. 왜 있잖아요. 좀 덤벙대는 애. 큰애 친구, 농구인가 한다는 애 말예요. 별소린 없구, 그저 안부 편지이긴 하지만 우스운 소리를 썼어요. 요새두 당신하고 꼭 붙어만 다니느냐구. 늙어서까지 그러면 다른 사람에게 남편이 공처가로 보이는 법이니까 조심하라구. 나 같으면 아마 죽을 지경일 거라구. 우스워 죽겠어…… 그렇게도 무뚝뚝하게만 보이던 남편의 표정에 미소가 어리는 것이 이런 얘기라도 하고 있는 모양이다. 그녀의 얘기는 그냥 계속된다. 작은애의 서독 여행은 괜찮았나 보죠. 이탈리아, 스페인, 스위스, 희랍까지 돌았다지만 돈이 모자라서 북구라파엔 못 갔던 것을 아쉬워하더군요. 이렇게 썼어요. 마마, 파파, 돈 좀 더 버세요. 다음 방학 때는 기어이 덴마크, 노르웨이, 스웨덴의 엽서를 뭉텅이로 마마, 파파에게 보낼 수 있도록. 알프스는 확실히 멋있어요. 희랍의 인상도 꽤나 큰 것이었지요.

his mouth, but he didn't seem to be smoking it. Jinsu kept waiting and waiting for him to take a drag on the pipe. *Come on, come on, guy, take a puff.* Jinsu felt more and more anxious. The man didn't look once at his wife; he kept his eyes fixed straight ahead, exuding the same dignified air Older Brother had had the previous evening. Finally he took a couple of deep drags on the pipe and then gently put his hand over the bowl. He remained impassive at the realization that it had gone out. He pulled a lighter from his pocket and relit the pipe. His wife had stopped talking and was quietly watching him. You could sense the intimacy that had developed between them over the years. But their closeness, like everything else, had something unfamiliarly Western about it. The comfort and ease with which they had had the good fortune to walk through life together was there for all to see. Only when bluish smoke began to rise from the pipe did his wife seem reassured. She started talking again, seemingly from where she had left off.

Our eldest is having stomach problems again. All he did was complain about his stomach in the letter we got yesterday from Harvard. Oh, yes, I forgot to tell you. We also got a letter from Freeman. You

나는 거기서 비로소 미국이라는 나라는 덩어리만 컸지 뿌리는 얕다고 실감으로 느낄 수 있었지요. 그것만으로도 큰 수확이 없지요. 미국은 어떤지 아세요? 좀 떠 있고 허황하고 알이 찬 맛이 없어요. 역시 몇 천 년의 전통을 지닌 나라는 비록 가난하더라도 부피가 있고 이편을 압도하는 것이 있어요. 그것은 중요한 것이지요. 우리들의 교양도, 우선 그런 것에 밑받쳐져 있어야 할 것 같아요. 겉만 핥지 말고 부박하지 말아야지요. 이번에 참 많이 배웠어요. 이렇게 제멋대로 응석을 부려둔 큰애보다는 자주성이 있고 단단하고 활달해서 사회에 나가더라도 빨리 익숙해질 것 같긴 해요. 아는 것도 빠르구. 어떻게 생각하세요, 당신은……? 참, 어제 대사 부인을 만났어요. 당신 안부를 묻더군요. 여전히 무뚝뚝하냐구, 무슨 멋으로 붙어 다니느냐구. 그래서 여전히 무뚝뚝하다고 대답해 줬지요. 그 부인의 조크는 좀 고급이야요. ICA의 그 누구인가 한 사람이 주관한…… 그 사람 이름이 뭐랬더라? 그 사람 좀 지저분하답디다. 엉큼한 사람이라고 말들이 많더군요. 자세한 내용은 모르겠지만, 어떻든 말이 많아요. 당신도 조심하세요. 올가미에 걸려들지 말구…… 그녀의 얘기는 그냥 계속되는데 이런 이야기라도 하고 있는 모양이었다.

36

know, that boy who has a mind of his own, the one who just does whatever he wants. Our son's friend, the boy who plays basketball. He didn't have much to say, just sent his regards, but there was one thing I found amusing. He asked if I was going to follow you around the world all the way into old age. He said we should be careful because people will think I've really got you under my thumb. He said it would drive him crazy if he got married and it turned out like that. Oh, gosh, I can't stop laughing...

The fact that even such a reserved, aloof man as her husband could not suppress a smile meant that in all likelihood these were the sorts of things she was saying. She started up again.

Looks like our youngest's trip to West Germany turned out okay. He made it to Italy and Spain and Switzerland, too, and also Greece. But he was really disappointed when he ran out of money and couldn't go to any of the northern European countries. Here's what he wrote in his letter: "Mom, Dad, make some more money, please. So when school's out again I can send you a whole pile of postcards from Denmark and Norway and Sweden. The Alps were fantastic. And Greece really left a deep impression on me. It made me realize for the first time that

진수는 입에 단침이 괴어와, 창문을 조금 열면서 뒤에 앉은 외국인 기자에게 열어도 괜찮겠느냐는 눈짓을 보냈다. 그는 어느새 졸고 있다가 화닥닥 상체를 일으키더니 덮어놓고 올라잇 올라잇, 털이 부숭부숭한 손까지 내혼들면서 좋다고 하였다.

진수는 조심스럽게 괸 침을 창밖에다 뱉어냈다.

순간 버스는 임진강을 넘어서고 있었다. 와당탕와당탕 거리며 다리를 건너는데, 처참하게 비틀어진 쇠기둥이 강으로 곤두박질을 하고 있고, 동강 난 철판때기가 삐뚜름히 걸려 있기도 하여, 비로소 판문점행이라는 처절하고도 뚜렷한 의식과 결부가 되어서 웬 노여움 같은 것이 울컥 치밀어 올랐다.

버스 안에서는 그렇게도 돋보이던 외국인들이었지만 정작 판문점에 이르자, 그 냄새와 단려한 기운이 푸석푸석 무너져 보였다. 누구나가 회 범벅 같은 얼굴로 꽤나 생소한 듯이 어리둥절해서 판문점 둘레를 돌기만 했다. 이것저것 덮어놓고 카메라의 셔터를 누르기도 했다.

버스 안에서 주책없이 지껄여대던 그 작자가 북쪽 경비병에게 카메라를 들이댔다가, 순간 저쪽에서 와락 눈을

America may be a big country, but it doesn't have any roots. That in itself was an important insight. Do you know what America is? A gigantic, insipid lump of nothing floating in midair. There are nations with thousands of years of history and tradition that are currently mired in poverty. But you'll find that they have a core, a solid base to build on that doesn't exist in the United States. This is a matter of crucial importance. We need to find a foundation, something we can use as a ground to develop our culture. It's high time we stopped viewing everything in such a careless, superficial way. I learned a lot from my trip." He's immature, but he's got more of an independent spirit than our eldest. He's got a strong, outgoing personality. He'll have no trouble making his way in the world. He picks up on things quickly. Don't you think so, dear?... Oh, by the way, I ran into the ambassador's wife yesterday. She asked how you were doing. Whether you were still so standoffish, and what fun do I get going everywhere with you. I told her you were still your same old aloof self. She's got quite the sense of humor, don't you think? Remember that party a few days ago? The one given by that person from the ICA... What was that guy's name? I heard he's not to be trusted. Everyone's say-

부릅뜨면서 돌아서니까 싱긋이 웃고는 그도 그냥 돌아섰다. 제 동료한테로 가서 턱으로 그 경비병을 가리키며 잔뜩 주눅 든 얼굴로 속삭이듯이 말했다.

"저 사람 화났어."

"누구?"

"저 쬐끄만 경비원 말이야."

그들은 잠시 한가하게 웃었다.

남편과 쉴 사이 없이 재잘거리던 그 늙은 여기자가 진수에게로 다가오더니 차이니즈는 어느 편에 앉았느냐고 물었다. 아마 저 안쪽에 앉은 세 사람일 것이라고 하니까, 겹겹하게 그편을 흘끗거리곤 생큐 하고 호들갑스럽게 지껄였다.

어느새 북쪽 기자들이 나와 있었다.

이편 사람들이거니만 여겼는데, 어딘가 다른 구석이 있어 찬찬히 살펴보니 나팔바지에 붉은 완장을 찼다. 피식피식들 웃으면서 우르르 어울려 들었다. 서로 낯이 익어진 사람들끼리 인사를 하는가 보았다.

"오래간만입니다."

땅딸막한 사람 하나가 이편 사람에게 이렇게 말했다.

"오우, 나왔어?"

ing he's a backstabber. I don't know the details, but there's a lot of talk about him. You should be careful. Don't fall for anybody's tricks...

She kept on talking, going on, no doubt, about things like this.

Jinsu felt a quantity of spit pooling in his mouth. He turned and cracked the window open, then gave the foreign reporter sitting behind him a look asking whether it was all right to open it all the way. The reporter was dozing off but immediately straightened up, waving his hairy hand a couple of times to give the okay.

Jinsu carefully spit through the window.

The bus was rattling its way across the bridge over the Imjin River. Iron rods and beams dangled from twisted metal supports grimly sticking up out of the water. Jinsu was overcome with the sinkingly clear realization that he really was headed toward Panmunjom. He could feel a knot of anger forming in his chest.

The foreigners were quite at ease on the bus. But their sense of assurance seemed to collapse when they arrived at Panmunjom. They appeared rather out of place, wandering around with confused looks

인사를 받은 이편 사람이 더 익숙한 투를 내며 반말지 거리로 받았다.

허풍이 섞인 우월감과 상대편에 대한 은근한 비아냥거림이 범벅이 된, 언뜻 보기에도 조금 냉랭했다.

"담배 피우기요?"

저편에서 나온 사람이 담배를 권하자,

"또 공세로군."

하고 이편 사람이 받았다. 그러면서도 권하는 대로 담배 한 대를 뽑았다.

"당신들은 그, 무슨 소리요? 공세 공세 하는데, 대체 알 아듣지 못할 소릴 헌단 말야."

저편 사람이 또 이렇게 말했다.

"이러지 말어. 괜히 능청 떨지 말구. 솔직히 탁 터놓고 말해."

이편 사람이 받았다.

"그 좋은 소리군. 그래, 솔직히 터놓구 말합시다."

저편 사람이 또 이렇게 말했다.

진수는 혼자 히죽이 웃었다.

'재미있군.'

그 광경을 멍청히 건너다보고 있던 외국인 여기자가 옆

on their faces. Then they started taking pictures of everything that came in sight.

The guy who had been going on mindlessly about Okinawa pointed his camera at a North Korean MP, who gave him a fierce look and turned abruptly on his heel. An uneasy smirk came over the reporter's face; he turned away and walked over to one of his colleagues.

"That guy's not happy," he whispered uncomfortably, nodding in the direction of the MP.

"Which one?"

"The shrimpy one over there."

The two of them let out a few empty chuckles.

The reporter who had been so engrossed in conversation with her husband on the bus walked over to Jinsu and asked where the Chinese were sitting. Jinsu pointed out three people inside one of the buildings and told her they were probably Chinese. She glanced quickly in that direction and loudly thanked him several times.

The North Korean reporters had arrived.

At first Jinsu thought they were part of the group from the South, but then it struck him that there was something different about them. A careful look revealed that they had wide-cut pants and were

에서 귓속말로 물었다.

"저 사람 지금 뭐라고 말해요?"

"미국 사람들은 다 나가라고 그러는군요."

"오우, 그래요? 무서워라."

그녀는 놀라운 듯이 중얼거렸다. 잠시 동안 그쪽을 뚫어지게 건너다보다가 뒤 어깨가 조금 밑으로 처져서 저편 남편 있는 쪽으로 걸어갔다. 남편에게 가서 그쪽을 가리키며 무엇이라고 중얼대자, 남편은 여전히 표정이 없이 그편을 흘끗 한 번 쳐다볼 뿐 그냥 외면을 하였다.

"누님 나오셨소? 우리 누님 나오셨군. 오랜만이외다. 어떻게, 장산 잘 되우?"

씽씽 바람이 이는 듯이 휘익 들어와, 허옇게 살이 찌고 굵은 검은 테 안경을 낀 사람 하나가 북쪽에서 나온 서른 살 남짓 되어 보이는 조금 덕성스럽게 펑퍼짐하게 생긴 여기자에게 이렇게 기차 바퀴 지나가는 듯한 소리로 말했다.

치마저고리를 입고 있어서 이편 여자인 줄 알고 있었는데, 자세히 보니 붉은 완장을 차고 있었다. 그녀는 두 눈이 감기게 웃으면서 반색을 했다.

"어이구, 여전하시구려. 로동자 농민들 피땀을 빨아서 피둥피둥해지셨군. 더 뻔뻔해지구."

wearing red armbands. Smiling, they walked up to where Jinsu and the others were standing. A number of the reporters from both sides seemed on familiar terms.

"I haven't seen you for some time," said a short, squat reporter from the North.

"Well look who's here," responded one of the reporters from the South in a casual, informal manner.

There was a frostiness to the exchange. Both sides seemed to be sneering at each other, each trying to put on a show of superiority.

"How about a smoke?" The reporter from the North held out a cigarette.

"Leading the charge again, huh?" said the reporter from the South. Nevertheless, he took the cigarette.

"Why are you guys always saying things like that? 'Leading the charge, leading the charge.' What are you talking about?"

"Come on, don't be like that. Let's cut the nonsense and put all our cards on the table."

"Well said. Let's tell it like it is."

This is really something. Jinsu smiled inside.

The older foreign woman, who had been standing beside Jinsu watching the exchange, asked in a

그녀는 이렇게 말하면서도 악수를 청하였다.

"허, 왜 이래. 만나자마자 또 공세문 곤란한데. 장산 좀 됐다 하구 우선 인사나 하고 봅시다레."

손을 잡으면서 안경잡이가 말했다.

"공센 무슨 공세라고 그래. 공세 혼살이 났는지 원, 지레 벌벌 떨기부터 하니 지은 죄가 단단히 있나 보군."

주위 사람들은 히죽히죽 웃었다. 외국 기자들도 그 오고 가는 표정만으로도 짐작이 가는 듯 피식피식 웃었다.

"우리 매부께서도 안녕하시구, 조카아이들도 다아 잘 있구요? 참, 시아버지 모시기 고생되지 않소? 무척 고생이 될 텐데. 난 누님 고생을 생각하문 밤잠도 제대로 못 자지 않수."

안경잡이가 또 말했다.

그녀는 손으로 입을 가리고 나오는 웃음을 겨우 참아냈다.

"당신은 왜 그렇게 허풍이 심하오? 배운 건 허풍만 배웠소?"

조금 전의 그 땅딸막한 사람이 그 사이로 비집고 끼여들었다.

"그래, 난 허풍만 배웠다. 당신은 실속만 차려서 그렇게

whisper, "What did he just say?"

"That the Americans should get out."

"Oh, really? That's scary," she muttered with a look of surprise. She gazed intently at the reporters from the North, then walked toward her husband, shoulders slumped. She pointed toward the reporters from the North and said something to him. The expression on her husband's face held steady as he glanced toward them.

A chubby, fair-skinned reporter from the South wearing glasses with thick black rims breezed his way to the front of the group.

"Older Sister, is that you? Hey, Older Sister's here. Long time no see. How's everything going?" he asked in a ringing voice. The woman he was addressing appeared a little over thirty. She was on the attractive side, with gentle, wholesome curves.

Jinsu had assumed she was from the South because she was dressed in traditional clothing. Looking closely, however, he could see her red armband. She scrunched her eyes up as she smiled, glad to see the reporter from the South.

"Haven't changed a bit, I see. Fatter than ever. Sucking the blood of the farmers and the urban pro-letariat. More shameless than ever." Still, she held

쬐끄매졌군. 딱하다, 딱해. 이런 젠장, 누님하고 마음대로 인사도 못 하겠군."

이편에서 간 사람들이 와르르 웃음을 터트리자, 그 땅딸막한 사람도 조금 쓰겁게 웃으면서 말했다.

"영 안 통하는군. 아주 썩어 문드러졌군. 정말 딱하오."

"정말 딱하우. 이런 것이 왈 유머라는 거야. 유머라는 말 배워줘? 모르지? 거기선 모를 거야. 설명해줘?"

마침 안에서 마악 회담이 시작되고 있어, 잠시 조용했다.

진수는 창턱에 두 팔을 걸치고 안을 들여다보았다.

"초면이신 것 같은데, 처음 나오셨지요? 안녕하세요?"

등 뒤에 상냥스러운 목소리가 들려 고개를 돌렸다. 빵 긋 웃는 낯빛이다. 눈알이 투명하게 샛노랗고 얼굴이 납작하고 기미가 끼고 그런대로 깜찍하게 생겨 있었다. 남색 원피스에 붉은 완장을 찼다. 예사 처녀가 예사 총각에게 흔히 하듯, 수줍음이 어린 웃음을 띠었다. '야, 요것 봐라' 하고 진수는 생각하면서도,

"네, 안녕하세요."

하고 받았다.

아리랑 담배를 피워 물면서 비스듬히 그녀 편으로 돌아섰다.

out her hand.

"Easy now. Before you go on the attack, how about a proper response to a proper greeting?" protested Black Rims as he shook hands with her.

"Attack? What's gotten into you, Mr. Defensive? You certainly do seem nervous—you wouldn't have something to hide, would you, something really awful perhaps?"

Everybody laughed. Even the foreign reporters who had been watching the exchange grinned as if they had guessed from the facial expressions what was being said.

"How's Brother-in-Law?" Black Rims carried on. "And the kids, my nieces and nephews? No trouble with Father-in-Law? You must be having a tough time. I can't sleep at night thinking about what you must be going through."

The woman covered her mouth with her hand, barely able to control her laughter.

"Why are you always such a windbag? Didn't you learn anything else in school?" interjected the short, squat reporter from the North.

"Nope. You, on the other hand, you're filled with real knowledge, the solid stuff. That's what turned you into such a midget. This is so ridiculous. Can't

"저, 서울에도 간밤에 비 많이 왔지요?"

그녀가 또 이렇게 물었다. '어렵쇼, 금니까지 하고.'

"네? 비 많이 왔지요?"

다시 그녀가 재우쳐 물었다.

"네."

"저, 어디 기자세요?"

"광명통신요."

"녜에, 그래요?"

진수는 가슴이 조금 후들거렸다.

마침 저편에서 조금 전의 그 안경잡이가 다시 큰 소리로 악악거렸다.

"이를테면 유머라는 것은 말이야, 당신들에게는 백번 죽었다가 깨도 알 수 없는 것, 사람이 제대로 사람 구실을 하기 시작해서 얼마쯤 더 있다 가야 서서히 알아지는 거란 말야, 알아? 알아듣겠어? 이렇게만 말해선 거긴 잘 모를 거야."

"여보, 지껄여도 침이나 튀지 않게 좀 지껄여."

"이런 젠장, 월사금을 받아두 시원치 않겠는데, 간섭이 왜 이리 심해. 이건 중요하니까 배워 둬요. 손해는 절대로 없을 테니까."

even ask after each other with my older sister."

The reporters from the South broke into peals of laughter. Even the short reporter from the North let out a sour chuckle.

"No way to get through to you, I guess. Rotten to the core. Utterly pathetic," he said.

"*I'm* pathetic? No, I'm being humorous. *Humor*— have you ever heard of the word *humor?* No, of course not. Do you want me to explain it to you?"

The meeting got under way inside the building, and everyone quieted down.

Jinsu rested his arms on the windowsill and peered inside.

"I don't believe we've met. Is this your first time here? How do you do?"

The voice was amiable and pleasant. Jinsu turned to see a soft smile playing across a woman's lips. Her eyes were clear and lively with a yellowish cast and her face was healthy-looking, with high cheekbones and a scattering of freckles. She was really quite cute. She was wearing a dark blue dress with a red armband. Her smile had all the bashfulness of a young, unmarried woman addressing a single man.

"How do you do?" responded Jinsu. *What have we*

진수는 발작적으로 폭소가 터져 나와 손으로 입을 가리며 키들키들 웃었다. 무언가 대번에 수월해지는 느낌이었다.

"참, 저런 사람을 어떻게 생각하세요?"

그녀가 미간을 조금 찡그리며 물었다.

"네? 어떻게 생각하세요?"

"글쎄, 사람 재미있지 않소."

진수는 그녀를 건너다보며 또 웃음이 터져 나오려는 것을 겨우 참았다. 그녀도 조금 웃는 듯하더니 일순 싸악 웃음이 벗겨지며 말했다.

"무엇이 덕지덕지 껴묻었어요. 그게 뭐냐 하면 실속 없이 곡예사 같은 몸짓만. 저런 걸 재미있다고 생각하는 건 이를테면 타락의 징조야요. 이럭저럭 와랑와랑 소음으로 속임수를 쓰는 거, 솔직하지가 못해요. 어떻게 생각하세요?"

'제법 지껄이는데.'

진수는 이렇게 생각했으나, 곧장 그녀의 말을 받았다.

"그렇지만 말요, 곡예사 같은 몸짓, 타락의 징조 운운하는데, 그것이 벌써 당신 머릿속의 어느 함정을 뜻하는 거죠. 당신들은 어떤 개개의 양상을 객관적인 큰 기준과의

here? He stuck an Arirang cigarette in his mouth.

"Did Seoul get a lot of rain last night too?" she asked.

What a cute gold tooth.

"Heavy rain, right?" she asked again.

"Yes."

"Which news agency are you with?"

"Gwangmyeong News."

"Oh, is that right?"

Jinsu felt a quiver inside.

Off to the side, Black Rims was back in action.

"Okay, let me tell you about humor. You guys are never going to get it. You could die, go to heaven, come back again, and you'd still never get it. The only way you'll ever comprehend what I'm saying is to start living a proper life. Understand? There's no explaining it to you, you're just too thick."

"Look, you can get worked up all you want, but at least stop spitting all over the place."

"Hey, I'm giving you a free lesson here, you ought to be paying me for this. Don't interrupt your teacher when he's telling you something important. You can learn from what I'm saying. Just be still and listen, it's not going to hurt."

Jinsu barely kept from breaking into laughter. He

관련 속에서만 포착하지만, 우리네에선 그렇지가 않아요. 저런 것이 비록 당신 말대로 속임수라고 쳐도 속임수치고는 즐겁고 순진한 것이라 그런 말이지요. 타락의 징조라는 것도 명확한 개념으로 간단히 처리될 성질은 아니지요. 어떤 분위기가 완숙의 경지에 이르러서 익어 터질 때, 이를테면 타락의 징조라는 게 나타나는데요. 전체적으로 포착하면 피상적으로 명료하지만, 그것만 고집하는 건 무리지요. 그런 방법은 유형을 가르기만 하는 데는 필요해도, 어떤 경우의 섬세한 진실은 포착 못 해요. 감은 더운 물에 넣어야 떫은 맛이 없어지지 않아요? 너무 오래 데우면 껍질이 벗겨지고 물큰물큰해지지요. 요컨대 타락의 징조 하는 것도 당사자의 경우에선 적당히 감미롭고 졸음이 오듯이 고소하고 팔다리를 주욱 펴고 있는 것같이 그래요."

"그건 비겁한 짓이야요. 그런 썩은 개인의 경우를 문제삼을 수는 없어요. 감은 익어서 먹으면 될 뿐이야요. 익는 과정을 운운하는 건 쓸데없는 사변이지요. 어떤 큰 가능성에 대한 큰 지향이 있어야 해요. 그렇지 않으면 그 찌뿌드드하게 졸음이 오는 감미에서 헤어나지 못해요. 사변에 매달리고 섬세한 경우에 매달리고 그러면 아무것도 못 해

covered his mouth and chuckled and felt a sudden sense of release.

"What's your opinion of that sort of person?" the woman asked with a tinge of a frown. When he didn't respond immediately, she repeated, "What do you think of someone like him?"

"Well, don't you think he's pretty funny?" Jinsu looked at her, still trying to stop himself from laughing. She smiled, as if she too were about to laugh. But then any hint that she might have been amused vanished from her face.

"It's like he's covered under layers of filth and grime. No, he's devoid of substance, maybe that's a better way to put it. He's like an acrobat, nothing but empty gestures. It's decadent to consider him funny. Ranting about all manner of things, manipulating words to deceive his listeners. Not very straightforward, is it? What do you think?"

She certainly has a thing or two to say.

"I beg to differ. You mention acrobat-like gestures, decadence. But this already shows the limits imposed on your mind. Your side grasps a variety of individual tendencies only in relation to an over-arching, objective standard. But we're different. You say he's manipulating words in order to deceive

요. 큰 결론만이 필요하지요. 이것이 바로 우리 현실의 정곡이야요. 어떻게 생각하세요? 그렇게 생각 않으세요? 참, 저 서울은 어때요?"

진수는 그녀의 현실 운운하는 말을 받으려다가 불쑥 튀어나오는 딴소리에 멈칫했다. 그러자 그녀는 웃으면서 말했다.

"그 문젠 알았어요. 그 문제에 대한 결론은 제가끔 얻으면 되잖아요? 제가 옳아요. 얘기도 효율적으로 속도 있게 합시다. 서울은 어때요?"

"……"

"네? 어때요?"

"평양은 어때요?"

"근사해요. 아주 굉장해요."

"서울두 근사하죠. 아주 굉장하고."

그녀가 피 하고 웃자, 진수도 피 하고 웃었다. 다음 순간 둘이 다 키들키들거렸다.

"가족이 전부 서울에 계시겠군요?"

그녀가 물었다.

"네."

진수가 대답했다.

people. Can't you see that it's all in fun? That there's actually a certain innocence to it? You can't simply declare something decadent and be finished with it. You have to consider the context. Only when a given circumstance has been taken to its logical extreme can one say that signs of decadence appear. If you consider everything in absolute terms, the world becomes superficially apparent. But it's unreasonable to insist on an approach like that. True, it can prove very useful when you're breaking everything down into categories and types, but then you'll never be able to grasp the truth that lies below the surface. You have to boil a persimmon to get rid of the sourness, right? But boil it too long and the skin comes off and it starts to stink. In other words, in any given situation, in any individual case, a certain amount of decadence is appropriate. Not too much, not too little. That's what adds flavor to life, gives a person that sweet, comfortable feeling you get right before you drop off to sleep."

"That's the kind of argument people make when they're afraid to face up to things. There's no need to pay so much attention to the individual case. When a persimmon's ready for eating, you eat it. What's the point of idle speculation about the

"결혼은 하셨어요? 실례지만."

그녀가 얼굴을 약간 붉히면서 또 이렇게 물었다.

"아뇨."

진수는 문득 엊저녁 형님 방으로 들어섰을 때, 웃저고리를 갈아입던 형수에게서 야한 냄새가 나던 일이 떠올랐다. 그는 조금 쓸쓸한 표정이 되었다.

"참, 저 남북 교류를 어떻게 생각하세요?"

그녀가 또 이렇게 물었다.

"네? 교류요? 글쎄…… 결국 이렇죠. 지금 당신하구 나하구 교류가 가능해지지 않았습니까? 참 간단하게…… 그러나 이런 걸 빗대어서 모든 것이 다 이런 투로 될 수 있다고 생각하는 건 지금 우리가 처해 있는 처지로서는 너무 소박하구 낙천적인 생각 같군요. 우리 남북 관계는 원체 착잡해요. 6·25 이전부터의 그 끔찍끔찍한…… 이 리얼리티를 리얼리티대로 포착하는 것이, 참 리얼리티라는 말은 모르겠군."

진수는 얘기가 신명이 나지 않아, 뜨적뜨적 이렇게 말하고는 씽긋 웃었다.

"사실주의의 그, 그것 말이지요?"

"네, 네, 그런 거요. 그런 것과 관련이 있는 문제거든요.

process it goes through to get ripe? We should always keep the big picture in mind. If you want to understand the society you're in, it's crucial to examine its overall structure. Otherwise you'll be lost forever. You'll never to break free from that 'sweet, comfortable feeling' of yours. You'll never accomplish anything if you insist on focusing on the minute details of each particular situation. What we need to do is draw our conclusions and set our goals accordingly. That's the reality confronting us. What do you think? Don't you agree? By the way, how's life in Seoul?"

Jinsu was about to offer a response to her mention of 'reality' but was thrown off guard by the sudden change of subject. She smiled at his hesitation.

"Let's drop it for now. Everyone should come to his own conclusions about this problem, don't you think? I do believe I'm right as far as that goes. Let's save time and discuss things in the most efficient manner possible. So how is life in Seoul?"

Jinsu said nothing.

"Well?"

"You first—how's life in Pyongyang?"

"Fantastic. It's really great."

"Seoul's fantastic too. Really great."

민족의 양식이라는 것도 현실적인 조건 앞에서는 당장 먹
혀들 여지가 없어요. 현실은 어떻게 해볼 도리가 없게 되
어 있지 않아요?"

　그녀가 달래듯이 말했다.

　"그렇지가 않아요. 조금도 복잡하지도 않아요. 지극히
간단하지요. 당신도 자기 운명을 자기가 쥐고 있다고 생
각하시지요? 그렇지 않으세요? 그렇지요? 그러니까 간단
하지요. 패배의식과 우유부단은 못써요. 문제는 간단한
걸 괜히 복잡하게 생각하려고 해요. 교류를 하면 교류가
되는 거야요."

　"그러나 피차 타산이 있지요. 그런 본질론이 통하지 않
아요. 그렇게 간단히 생각하는 건 당신들의 상투적인 경
우이고, 이편 경우는 또 이편 경우거든요. 이편 경우의 내
력이 또 있어요. 철저한 현실주의가 작용하는 거지요. 막
하는 말로, 먹느냐 먹히느냐 하는 측면 말이지요. 우리,
조금 더 얘기가 솔직해져야 하겠군요."

　그러나 그녀는 두 눈을 깜짝깜짝했다.

　"누가 먹고 누가 먹히나요? 그 발상법부터가 비뚤어진
생각이야요. 요컨대 피할 까닭은 없어요. 어떻게 생각하
세요. 정치의 표준이란 걸 두고 계시나요? 어느 특정된 개

The woman laughed, and Jinsu followed suit. The two of them found themselves chuckling together.

"Do all your family live in Seoul?"

"Yes."

"I'm sorry to be so forward, but could I ask if you're married?" She blushed ever so slightly.

"No, I'm not."

Jinsu recalled entering Older Brother's room the night before and encountering the lascivious smell coming from Sister-in-Law as she was changing her blouse. A wry expression came over his face.

"What's your opinion regarding the exchange taking place between North and South?" she asked.

"Exchange? Oh, right, sorry. Well, I guess we could think of it like this. Aren't you and I engaged in an exchange right now? That part of it's easy enough... But of course it would be much too simplistic, too optimistic, to think that what we're doing now could serve as an example for the sort of tone that should be adopted in the discussions. The relations between North and South are so very complex. The situation prior to the outbreak of the Korean War, I mean... To understand this horrendous 'reality' in and of itself—oh, I forgot, you wouldn't know the English term *reality*, would

인의, 혹은 집단의, 감정적인 장애라든가, 타성에서 오는 고집이라든가, 우선 그런 건 제거되어야 하지 않아요? 선택할 권리는 묻혀서 사는 일반에게 있어요. 그 사람들에게 선택할 기회와 자유를 주어야 해요."

그녀는 얼굴이 붉어지면서 좀 강렬한 어조로 이렇게 말했다. 진수가 응했다.

"그렇지요. 선택할 자유를 주어야지요. 아무렴요. 당신들은 줍니까? 당신들 세계에서 자유라는 건 어떤 모습을 지니는가요? 자유조차 혹시 강제당하는 건 아닌지요? 설령 그것이 당신들이 말하는 진보적 민주주의가 표방하는 선택된 몇 사람의 미래에 대한 일정한 역사적 전망에 안받침된 옳은 강제라고 가정하더라도 말이지요. 어때요, 거기서 견딜 만해요? 솔직히 말하세요."

진수는 조금 신랄한 데를 찌른 듯하여 씽긋 웃었다.

순간 그녀는 발끈했다.

"신념이 문제지요. 자유는 허풍선과 같은 허황한 것일 수가 없어요. 자유의 진가는 그 사회 나름의 일정한 도덕적 규범과 인간적 품위와 결부가 되어서 비로소 제대로 설 수 있는 거지요. 자유 이전에 정의가 있어요. 그렇지 않으면 자유는 이용만 당해요. 빛 좋은 개살구지요. 우리

you?" Jinsu asked abruptly with a smile, aware that he wasn't making much sense.

"The facts as they are—actuality—right?"

"Exactly. The whole problem hinges on that. It makes appealing to such things as national customs seem meaningless. Don't you agree that we're faced with a reality that's nearly impossible to overcome?"

"Not necessarily. There's nothing overly complicated about the situation. It's rather simple, actually. Don't you think you're in charge of your own destiny? Don't you? You are, right? That's what makes it so simple. There's no room for a defeatist attitude, for indecision. The problem is when people take a simple situation and make it complicated for no good reason. You engage in an exchange and that's it, you've got yourself an exchange," she said in a soothing tone.

"But each side comes to the table with its own agenda. You can't just assume that no calculation has gone into any of it. Your side makes use of the commonplace notion that things should be approached simply, but our side is different. And our side has its reasons for taking such a position. That's where cold, hard reality comes into play. I'm talking about survival of the fittest, to eat or be

모랄의 기본이 뭣인지 아세요? 우리 민족의 나갈 바 큰 방향이야요. 개인은 거기 제대로 째어들어 있어야만 해요. 그 속에서 자유야요. 결국 이념이 문제겠군요. 당신의 생각은 나태 그것이야요. 타락되고 싶다는 말밖에, 놀고 싶다는 말밖에 아니야요. 자유에 대한 옳은 인식도 없고, 일정한 이념도 없고, 있는 것은 그날그날의 동물적인 희뿌연 자기밖에 없어요. 비트적거리고 주저앉고 싶은 자기……."

"그럼 자기를 팽개치고 무엇이 남아요. 놀고 싶고 적당히 나쁜 짓 하고 싶은 자유란 최고급이지요. 사람은 원래 그렇게 생겨 먹었어요. 그것을 크나큰 관용으로써 받아들일 수 있는 사회가 있어요. 부피와 융통이 있는, 그런 것이 적당히 용서가 되면서도 전체로 균형이 잡혀 있는. 참, 어느 것이 허풍선이냐 따질까요? 자기조차 팽개쳐 버린 이념 덩이가 허풍선이냐, 그렇지 않으면 적당히 자기를……."

"천만에, 자기가 없이 어떻게 이념이 있을 수 있어요. 자기를 왜 팽개쳐요. 완벽하고 명료한 자기는 이념에 밑받침되어 있어야 해요. 그렇지 않고는 흐늘흐늘하고 비트적거리는 자기의 검불만 남아요. 당신의 자유에 대한 견

eaten. We have to start being more frank with each other."

The woman blinked in astonishment. "So it's all about who eats and who gets eaten? The way you frame the issue is just plain distorted. Let's tackle the problem head-on, okay? What sort of standard do you think should be set for politics? Don't you think that above all else we need to eliminate what you might call the sentimental attachment—or, to put it another way, the force of habit, the inertia— that allows for the privileging of a particular individual or group? The right to choose belongs to the common people, those who toil in obscurity. They must be given the opportunity and the freedom to choose," she declared fervently, turning red with excitement.

"I agree. They must be given the right to choose. No doubt about that. Does your side give it to them? What form does freedom take in your world? Have you ever considered the possibility that freedom has become just another one of the things you foist upon the people? It doesn't matter whether you want to regard such coercive measures as necessary, justified by the predetermined historical trajectory of your so-called progressive democracy, the one pro-

해는 썩어빠진 거야요. 한마디로 썩어빠진 거야요. 쉰 냄새가 나요. 곰팡이 냄새가…… 어마아, 그런 논리가 어디 있어요?"

"있지요, 있구말구. 사람이 지니고 있는 내면의 부피와 깊이는 한이 없어요. 당신들은 사람도 어떤 효율의 데이터로만 간주하고 있어요. 당신들 사회에서 옳다 그르다 하는 그 기준이 대개 짐작이 되는데, 일면적인 거지요."

"아니야요, 다만 지금 우리들의 현실이 다급해 있다뿐이지요. 원인은 그것이야요."

"참 도스토옙스키나 셰익스피어를 아시오? 어떻게 생각하시요?"

"알아요. 도스토옙스키는 약간 자신을 희화화하여 놓고 필요 이상으로 비장한 몸짓을 하는 도시 소시민의 사변철학이고, 셰익스피어는…… 시민사회가 싹트기 시작하는 사회의 여러 모를 부피 있게 부각시켰어요."

"무서운 추상이로군."

"아니야요, 본질이 그래요. 세부에 구애되지 말고 큰 윤곽으로 포착해야 해요."

마침 좀 전의 외국인 여기자가 옆으로 지나가고 있었다.

jected by the chosen few. How about it? Is life bearable in the North? I'd appreciate an honest answer." Jinsu grinned, as if he had got her where it hurt.

"It's a question of conviction. *Freedom* is not a word to be bandied about by someone full of hot air. The true value of freedom emerges only in a society that has established ethical standards that take human dignity into account. Justice comes before freedom. Otherwise freedom becomes nothing more than a tool to be manipulated. Like an apple that's shiny and red on the outside but rotten to the core on the inside. Do you know what our basic moral position is? Our concern is with mapping out the future direction for the entire nation. The individual must find a place within this concern. That's where freedom lies. I guess in the final analysis it does come down to ideology. Apathy, indifference—that's the only way to describe your way of thinking. What you mean to say is that all you want to do is play around, engage in all sorts of depraved activities. You have no proper concept of freedom, you have no ideology. What you've got is your animal urges. That's what's leading you from one day to the next. That's what the 'self' you want to revel in is made of, your staggering, aimless

'오우, 원더풀.' 히죽 웃으면서 이런 표정을 했다.

그리하여 잠시 얘기가 끊겼다. 조금 뜸하다 했더니, 조금 전에 요란스럽게 지껄이던 안경잡이와 그 '누님'께서는 같이 사진을 찍고 있었고 둘 다 키들키들 웃고 있었다. 회담 장소 건너편 쪽 처마 밑에서는 양쪽 사람들 대여섯 명이 우르르 붙어서 실랑이질을 하고 있었다. 들여다보이는 회담장은 바야흐로 서릿바람의 도가니였다. 납치한 어부들을 당장 송환하라는 것이었다. 기본 내용을 알아서 그런지 말소리는 들리지 않고 그저 스피커 소리가 귀에 윙윙하기만 했다. 저편은 울부짖고 이편은 전혀 무관심의 표정이고, 이편이 울부짖으면 저편 얼굴에 하나같이 비아냥거림이 어리고, 드디어 저편에서 책상을 두드리고, 순간 맞은편에 앉은 이편 사람은 시끄럽구먼 왜 이리 야단이여, 이쯤 조금 어리둥절한 낯색을 하고, 비로소 스프링 달린 쇠붙이 의자를 한번 들썩이고 헛기침을 하고, 똑똑히 들으란 말이여, 별로 쓸모 있는 소리는 아니지만, 이렇게 미리 다지기라도 하듯이 상대편을 일순간 맞바로 쏘아보고, 내리읽고…… 이번엔 스피커에서 영어가 울리고 서릿바람이 일고…… 이런 연속이다.

"인도적인 원칙으로서도 돌려보내 줘야지."

self..." Her voice trailed off in anger.

"What's left after you throw away the self? The highest form of freedom is the one that allows people to play around a little, to commit a few harmless misdeeds. That's the way people are—it's human nature. There are societies that make the necessary allowances for this. These societies possess both depth and adaptability. They are appropriately tolerant of such behavior while maintaining an overall balance and stability. Does that line of reasoning make me full of hot air? Who's full of hot air, someone who throws away a sense of self and becomes nothing more than an ideological abstraction, or someone who, appropriately—"

"By all means, you're right. How can there be ideology without the self? Why throw away the self? The point is, one must take a firm, clear sense of self and ground it in the proper ideology. Otherwise, you're nothing but the empty shadow of a person, wandering around without a purpose. Your view of freedom is rotten to the core. It's got a putrid smell. It reeks... How can you possibly try to justify yourself in such a way?"

"It's possible. Completely possible. There's no limit to the depths of the inner self. Your side only thinks

잠시 말없이 안을 들여다보던 그녀가 진수 들으라는 듯
이 혼잣소리처럼 말했다.

"아가씨, 몇 살이오?"

진수가 조금 전의 억양과는 달리 단호하게 물었다. 여
자가 너무 까불면 못써, 제법 이런 눈짓으로 숙성한 남자
의 그 위엄을 드러내면서.

"스물넷요."

그녀는 약간 놀라면서 진수를 쳐다보곤 조금 당황해 하
며 겁에 질린 듯이 대답했다.

'다섯 살 차이라……' 진수는 익살을 부리듯 이렇게 생
각하며,

"조금 수월해집시다. 피곤해질 소리만 하지 말구. 언어
는 언어 이상을 뛰어넘을 수 없거든. 우리들의 현실이 바
로 그거란 말요. 비겁한 도피 의식이라고 해도 할 수는 없
지만. 어떻든 피차 타산이 앞선 거래가 아닙니까. 좋은 소
리 해보아야 믿을 사람도 없구. 이쯤 되지 않았소? 비극이
랄밖에요."

하자, 그녀는 잠시 어리둥절한 낯색으로 다시 이 말을 받
으려고 했다. 그러나 진수가 그녀를 막았다.

"이를테면 말요, 내가 남편이고 당신이 아내라고 칩시

of people in terms of data to be made use of in the most efficient manner possible. I'm getting a feel for just how one-dimensional the moral standards are in your society."

"No. It's just that right now we're confronted with some pressing circumstances. That's the reason for it."

"Have you heard of Dostoevsky or Shakespeare? What do you think of them?"

"Of course I'm aware of them. Dostoevsky inserts a characterized version of himself in his novels. His emphasis on the unnecessarily grandiose gestures made by the urban petit bourgeoisie places his work in the category of speculative philosophy. As for Shakespeare, he offers an incisive portrayal of the various aspects of a country in which the sprouts of civil society are first appearing."

"That's frighteningly abstract."

"No, that's the essence of it. One shouldn't get hung up on particulars. You have to grasp the over-all framework."

The older foreign woman walked by; the smile on her face seemed to say, *How wonderful.*

They stopped talking. A calmness seemed to come over them. Black Rims was having his picture taken

다. 그럴듯한 놀음이 제법 될 것 같지 않소? 이편에서 위엄을 부리는 것과 그편에서 아양을 떠는 것이 제법 썩 들어맞을 것도 같은데. 이편에서 눈을 부라리면 제법 수그러질 줄도 알긴 알 것 같고, 이편에서 술이나 마시고 조금 흐트러진 표정으로 우자우자하면 그쪽에서는 제법 기승을 세울 줄도 알긴 알 것 같고, 이편에서 노래를 부르면 시늉으로라도 반주쯤도 하겠고, 양말짝이나 기저귀 빠는 것도 못할 일 아니겠고, 애에게 젖 물리는 것도 제격이겠고, 어떻소? 헌데 스물넷이면 노처녀군."

대뜸 물 쏟아 버리듯이 진수가 말하자, 어머나아 하듯 그녀는 입을 조금 헤벌린 채 멀거니 진수를 쳐다보았다. 다음 순간 한 손으로 입을 가리고 키들키들 웃었다.

"천만의 말씀이오. 스물넷이 뭣이 노처녀예요?"

하고 익살을 섞으며 그녀도 받았다. '어렵쇼' 하고 진수는,

"여자 스물넷이면 노처녀야. 알아둬. 거기서는 버릇이 그런가. 버릇치고는 못됐군. 스물넷에 시집도 못 가면 쓰레기 취급을 당하는 거야 알아둬."

하자 그녀는 정신을 차리려는 듯이 조금 새침해졌다. 순간 주위를 휘딱 살폈다. 누가 들으면 이건 좀 창피하군,

with his "older sister." The two of them were laughing, the earlier fuss apparently forgotten. Meanwhile, half a dozen reporters from both sides were bickering beneath the eaves of the building where the meeting was taking place.

Inside, the atmosphere was frosty. One camp was demanding the immediate return of a group of fishermen detained by the other. Jinsu knew the gist of the matter and didn't bother trying to make out the words emanating from the loudspeaker, which in any case were lost in the static beating against his ears. Those sitting nearest Jinsu would express their outrage while their counterparts across the table maintained expressions of utter indifference. The group on the far side would then proceed to rant and rave only to be met with looks of haughty disdain. The near side, in turn, would pound the table while their antagonists gaped in amazement as if to say, *Calm down. Why are you getting so riled up?* Finally all would lean back in their reclining metal office chairs, clear their throats, stare fiercely across at the opposition as if ordering them to listen carefully, and then look down again. English would issue from the loudspeaker, a chill would come over the room, and then the cycle would start all

약간 난처해 하는 표정이 되었다. 그러나 다시 받았다.

"말솜씨가 역시 망종 냄새가 나요. 거기선 남자 구실을 하려면 그래야 되나요?"

"망종이라니, 무슨 소리야? 못 알아들을 소린데."

"망할 종자, 이를테면 망나니, 어깨, 깡패……"

"그럼 꽁생원만 사냔가, 거기선?"

"천만에."

"그럼 됐어."

'정말 그럼 됐어.' 진수는 속으로 뇌까리면서 되씹었다. '그럼 됐어. 힘들 것 없어.'

어느새 먹구름이 잔뜩 끼어 있었다. 어두워졌다. 내다 보이는 좁은 들판으로 소나기가 몰려오고 있었다. 먼지 없는 바람이 일었다. 먹구름 틈 사이로 삐져서 내리붓는 흰 햇살이 빛기둥이 되어 동편 산 틈바구니로 곤두서 있었다. 그곳만 무지갯빛으로 환했다. 그 아롱아롱한 빛무더기가 간접으로 엇비치어 판문점 둘레는 마치 새벽녘 같아졌다. 그것이 무척 신선하면서도 이역의 분위기를 돋우었다. 사람들은 어느 틈 사이로 빛줄이 새어 들어오는 어두운 움 속에라도 들어 있는 것 같은 무르익음에 잠겨 있

over again.

Looking on with Jinsu, the woman broke her silence. "Those fishermen should be returned on humanitarian grounds," she muttered, loud enough for Jinsu to hear.

"How old are you, miss?" Jinsu asked, firming his tone of voice. His eyes flashed with a mature, masculine dignity that said, *A woman shouldn't be so uppity.*

The woman tried to appear nonplussed, but the look she gave Jinsu was confused and frightened. "I'm twenty-four."

So there's a five-year difference. Jinsu smiled to himself. "Let's lighten up and stop wearing each other down. Words don't solve anything—they just lead to more words. That's the reality of our situation. You can call me a coward, say I'm running away—but there's nothing I can do about that. Anyway, doesn't each side come to the table just to further its own agenda? No matter how well one side makes a case for itself, the other side's not going to believe it. Isn't that the point we've reached? It's a tragedy. No other word for it."

She was at a loss. Before she could respond, Jinsu continued.

었다. 제각기 무엇인가에 취해 있는 느낌이었다. 환한 날빛 밑에서는 웅성대는 소리가 밝은 기운을 띠었었으나 하늘이 꽉 막히자 그 소리들은 한데 엉겨 안으로만 덩어리가 되어 달려들었다. 드디어는 그것이 흥건하게 익어 독을 뿜었다.

"비가 오려나 보다, 비가."

누구인가 이렇게 혼자소리로 지껄였다. 북쪽 사람인지 남쪽 사람인지 알 수가 없었다. 그러나 사람들은 그런 소리쯤 그냥 흘려 버리고 말았다.

"오우, 원더풀."

어느 구석에서 이런 소리가 또 들렸다.

동편 쪽에 세로 섰던 빛기둥도 어느새 사라지고 더욱 어두워졌다. 비로소 사람들은 조용조용히 하늘을 올려다보고 혹은 들판을 내다보았다. 그러면서 갑자기 수선대었다.

드디어 빗방울이 들더니 금방 연이어서 장대 같은 소나기가 쏟아지기 시작했다.

함석지붕이 와당와당 와라랑 하자 울부짖던 스피커 소리가 멀어졌다. 대뜸 땅 위엔 보얀 빗물 안개가 서리고 하늘과 땅이 그대로 굵은 물줄기로 이어졌다. 순간 회담 장소 안에 앉은 사람들도 일제히 밖을 내다보며 눈이 휘둥

"I have an idea. Let's assume that I'm the husband and you're the wife. How about it? I'll put on a stately, dignified air and you'll giggle and make eyes at me. That would be perfect. If I give you an angry look, you'll know you'd better be careful. If I've had a few drinks and start holding forth, you'll know what to do. If I start singing, you'll at least make a show of chiming in. You'll wash the socks and the diapers. And you'll be just fine at breast-feeding. How about it? Twenty-four makes you an old maid, you know." The words gushed from Jinsu's mouth.

The woman stared at him slack-jawed, then began to laugh, covering her mouth.

"Sorry, but no thanks. Twenty-four and I'm an old maid?" she joked.

Well, well, look at that. "You'd better believe it. Twenty-four equals old maid. What, that's not the way it is where you live? Then something's wrong. If you can't get married by twenty-four, you're considered trash. Remember that."

She drew back, suddenly self-conscious, and took a quick, embarrassed look around. Was she worried someone might overhear their conversation?

"You sound like a desperado. Where you're from, is that the way you prove you're a man?"

그레졌다. 굉장한 소나기군, 모두 이렇게라도 생각하는가 보았다. 그 놀랍게도 일률적인 표정이 기묘한 역설을 느끼게 했다. 늘어선 경비병들이 처마 밑으로 피해 서고, 둘레에 서 있던 사람들도 하나둘 이리저리 엇갈리며 괴이한 소리를 내지르면서 막사로 뛰기 시작하였다. 그 필사적인 분위기가 전염이 되어 모두가 와르르 헤쳐지는 속에 진수도 덥석 그녀의 손을 잡았다. 그녀는 화닥닥 놀라 손을 잡힌 채 같이 뛰었다. 앞에 지프차가 가로서 있었다. 진수는 그 문을 열고 먼저 그녀를 올려 앉혔다. 그녀도 같이 뛰는 사람이 누구인지도 딱히 모르고 덮어놓고 올라탔다. 진수는 지프차에 올라타자 문을 닫고 문고리를 잠갔다. 순간 그녀는 문을 열고 와락 나가려고 하였으나, 진수가 그녀의 손을 다시 잡았다. 그녀는 얼굴이 무섭게 일그러지며 사무친 애걸조로 진수를 바라보았다.

"안심해, 그편 차니까."

진수가 말했다.

그녀는 무슨 암시나 받은 것처럼 일순 활짝 피어나듯이 웃었다. 그러나 사실은 진수도 아직 어느 쪽 차인지 알지 못했다.

"이봐."

"Desperado? What's a desperadpo?"

"You know, a criminal, a gangster, a hoodlum..."

"You mean all the men up there are a bunch of cold fish?" Jinsu asked.

"No, not at all."

"Then that's that." *Yes, indeed, the matter's settled,* Jinsu thought. *The matter's settled. Nothing to it.*

Storm clouds had suddenly obscured the sky. Darkness settled over the surroundings. A rain shower began to work its way up from the narrow stretch of fields below. A clear, dust-free wind kicked up. And then a column of pale sunlight seeped through a crack in the cloud cover, stretching its way down to the mountains to the east. A rainbow appeared, bathing the mountains in its colors. Red patches of light found their way over to Panmunjom, lighting up the area as if it were dawn. There was a freshness in the air, but also an eerie sense of alienation. It was as if everyone were undergoing fermentation, buried in a dark storage cellar with splinters of light poking through. All seemed to have entered a trancelike state. Their voices had rung vibrantly when the sun was out, but now that the sky was filled with clouds, their

진수가 불렀다.

"……"

그녀는 조마조마해 하였고, 쌔근쌔근 숨을 몰아쉬며 말했다.

"이북 가시죠? 네? 이북 가시죠?"

"이봐, 금니 어디서 했어?"

"네……?"

그녀는 한 손으로 입을 가렸다.

"금니 어디서 했어?"

눈을 부릅뜨며 진수가 다시 물었다.

"평양에서요."

"입 벌려 봐."

"싫어요."

"가족이 몇이야?"

"일곱요."

"누가 벌어먹여?"

그녀는 비로소 키들거리듯이 웃었다.

"그렇게 물으면 곤란해요. 우리에게선 벌어먹구 자시구가 없어요."

"참 그렇겠군."

words seemed to curl up into little balloons and tumble back inside their mouths. And then the balloons burst, releasing a noxious smell.

"Looks like rain. Yes, it does," someone muttered to himself. A Southerner? A Northerner? No way to tell. Everyone seemed to ignore him, letting the remark wash itself away.

"How wonderful," someone said in English.

The column of light in the mountains to the east disappeared and the darkness shrouding the surroundings became a shade deeper. Everyone regarded the sky then looked down at the fields. And all at once they were chattering loudly.

Finally a few drops of rain, which suddenly became a downpour. The rain spattering on the galvanized-iron roof of the building where the meeting was taking place drowned out the shouting that had been coming through the speaker. In no time a heavy mist covered the ground; earth and sky were linked by thick streams of rain. Everyone at the conference table looked outside, wide-eyed, marveling at the cloudburst. The startlingly identical expressions on their faces gave rise to an odd, paradoxical feeling. The MPs, who had been standing in single file, retreated beneath the eaves; one by one, peo-

그녀가 비에 젖은 머리를 쥐어짰다. 신 살구알 냄새가 났다.

"살구알 냄새가 난다."

"네?"

그녀가 짜던 손을 잠시 멈추었다.

"살구알 냄새가 나, 네 머리에서."

"이북 가시죠? 네?"

거친 숨소리로 또 물었다.

"데리구 가봐."

그녀는 조심스럽게 바깥을 살폈다.

그러나 여전히 줄기차게 퍼붓는 빗속에 밝은 칠흑의 어둠 같은 무색의 공간으로 차 있을 뿐이었다.

"데리고 가봐."

진수가 또 말했다.

"답답하군요, 답답해요. 어떡해야 좋을지 모르겠군요. 이런 경우엔 순서가…… 아이, 빈 왜 이리 쏟아질까. 보세요, 용기를 내세요, 네? 용기를 내요."

"이봐."

"……"

"이봐."

ple made a beeline toward the tents, letting out odd noises as they ran. Caught up in the frenzy of all these people plunging through the torrents of water, Jinsu grabbed the young reporter. Startled, she ran with him, hand in hand. There, a jeep. Jinsu opened the door and ushered her in. She seemed not to have realized it was him. Jinsu jumped in behind her and locked the doors. She tried to open the door and get out, but Jinsu seized her hand again. She gave him a desperate, pleading look, her face twisted in a painful knot.

"Relax. The car belongs to your side," Jinsu said. In truth, he didn't know which side the jeep belonged to.

She broke into a broad smile, as if she'd taken a hint.

"Hey," said Jinsu.

She didn't respond right away.

She was nervous, on edge. "You want to come up north, right? Is that it? You'd like to come up north?" she asked hurriedly, taking deep breaths.

"Look, where'd you get that gold tooth?"

"Sorry?" She covered her mouth.

"The gold tooth—where'd you get it?" Jinsu asked again, glaring at her fiercely.

"아이, 이러지 말아요. 이러문 못써요."

"남자 여자가 이렇게 아무도 없이 단둘이 마주 앉아 있으면 어떤지 알지? 그런 그리움을 그리워해 보았나?"

"아이, 이러문 못써요."

그녀는 와들와들 떨며, 떨리는 두 손을 들어 얼굴을 가렸다. 손가락 사이로 겁에 질린 두 눈이 뚫려 있었다.

"이것 보세요."

그녀가 마지막 안간힘을 쓰듯이 불렀다.

"왜?"

"전 지금 할 일이 있어요. 해야 할 일이 있어요. 도와주세요, 네? 이건 분명히 우리 차지요. 그렇죠? 작정하세요. 어떻게 하실래요? 난 설득을 해야 해요. 어떻게 하실래요?"

"그래, 설득시켜 봐라. 어서 설득시켜 봐."

"우선 본인이 결정하세요. 그게 선차예요."

"지금 넌 놓여난 기분을 느끼지 않나? 너나 나나 마찬가지야. 놓여난 기분을 느껴야 돼."

"그런 얘기를 할 때가 아니야요, 지금은."

"이런 것이 우리 경우에서의 자유라는 거다, 겨우 이런 것이. 무엇인가, 고삐를 풀어 팽개친 연후에 겨우 남는 것

"In Pyongyang."

"Open your mouth."

"No."

"How many people in your family?"

"Seven."

"Who's the breadwinner?"

She laughed in spite of herself. "It's irrelevant—that's not the way we do things in our system."

"Oh, yeah, that's right."

She squeezed the water out of her hair. It smelled like a sour apricot. Jinsu told her as much.

"Excuse me?" She stopped squeezing her hair.

"Your hair smells like an apricot."

"You *would* like to come up north, right?" She was still breathing heavily.

"So take me."

She peered cautiously outside.

The rain continued to stream down. Everything was enveloped in a heavy darkness.

"Well?" Jinsu repeated.

"Oh, my, I can't think straight. What should I do? What's the first thing I'm supposed to do in this kind of situation? Why does it keep pouring like this? Whatever you do, don't lose your nerve, all right? Now's the time to dig down deep for every-

이 이런 거야. 그렇게 느끼지 않나? 이런 말은 여전히 썩은 소리라고만 생각하나?"

"이건 썩은 냄새야요. 분명히 썩은 냄새야요. 이런 건 끝까지 경계해야 해요. 전 그래야 해요."

그녀는 뭍에 나온 물고기처럼 발작이나 하듯이 울기 시작했다.

형님 방으로 들어섰다. 형님은 더블베드에 벌렁 누웠다가 천천히 일어났다. 불빛이 환하다.

형수는 잠든 조카를 안은 채 필요 이상으로 표정을 과장하면서 웃었는데, 어디가 어떻다고 쏘옥 집어낼 수는 없이 또 불결한 냄새가 났다.

"어때? 재미있었니?"
하고 형님이 물었다.

"끔찍스럽지 않았어요? 하긴 마찬가지 조선 사람이긴 했겠지만."

형수도 이렇게 곁다리 끼듯이 말했다. 진수는 멋쩍게 조금 웃었다.

"괜찮더군요. 구경할 만하더군요."

"사람들은 어떻든?"

thing you have."

"Hey."

No response.

"Hey!"

"Don't talk down to me like that. It's highly improper."

"Do you know what happens when a man and a woman are alone together like we are now? Haven't you ever had a hankering for that?"

"You shouldn't do this. It's not proper." Shaking violently, she covered her face with both hands. Her frightened eyes peeped out at him between her fingers. "I—I would like to tell you something," she stammered, as if mustering all of her remaining courage.

"What?"

"I have a duty to perform here. It's something I have to do. You can help me, can't you? This is our car, right? Please make a decision. What would you like to do? Tell me and I'll help you make up your mind. What do you want to do?"

"Sure, go ahead and try to convince me. Give it your best shot."

"You have to decide for yourself first."

"Don't you feel a sense of liberation? It has to be

형님이 또 물었다.

"뭐 그저……."

대답하기가 힘들어 우물쭈물 넘겼다.

형님은 조금 비아냥거리는 듯한 웃음을 입가에 흘리었다. 하긴 아랫사람 앞에서 저런 종류의 조금 얕보는 듯한 웃음을 웃는 것은 권위의 담을 쌓는 데 도움이 되기는 할 거라 하고 진수는 생각하는데, 어느새 형님은 딴청을 부리며 형수에게 물었다.

"와이셔츠 대려 놨나?"

"네, 10분이나 기다렸대나 봐요. 세탁소가 어찌나 붐비는지. 기집애(식모아이를 가리키는 말이었다), 안 됐으면 좀 있다가 갈 것이지 잔뜩 늘어붙어 앉아서. 덕분에 찾아오긴 했지만."

하고 형수는 진수를 건너다보면서 약간 이죽대었다.

"낼 전무가 미국 가. 비행장까지 나가 봐줘야지. 당신은 어떡할라우? 나가 보는 것이 좋겠는데."

형님이 또 말하였다. 형수는 얼굴빛이 대뜸 상기되면서 치맛바람을 일으키는 표정이 되었다.

"얼마 동안이나 가 있을라는지, 그 언니 또 속깨나 타겠군. 혼자선 못 견뎌 하는 걸. 그 언니 참 요새 다이아 반지

the same for both of us. You must feel it."

"This isn't the time."

"It *is* the time, and the opportunity, for us, for freedom. This is what freedom means for us. How can I put it—it's the feeling you get when you break free, when you cast off all restraints. You don't feel it? You still think I'm talking like a depraved man?"

"It *is* depraved. And it *is* totally rotten. This is what one has to guard oneself against at all costs. I can't allow it to get to me." She began to sob violently, wrenching herself back and forth like a fish flopping on the ground.

Older Brother was sprawled out on the double bed as Jinsu entered. He got up slowly. The room was brightly lit.

Holding her sleeping baby in her arms, Sister-in-Law produced an exaggerated smile. An unchaste smell once again pervaded the room. It was hard to say exactly where it was coming from.

"Well, how was it? Interesting?" Older Brother asked.

"Wasn't it just frightful?" Sister-in-Law chimed in. "But they are Korean after all, same as us, I suppose."

를 스리맞았답디다. 원, 반지두 스리를 당하나. 그 언닌 원체 정신이 산만해서. 헌데 참 몇 시에 떠나우? 언니두 며칠 못 만났는데 마침 잘됐수."

그러나 형님은 다시 딴청을 피우며 가볍게 하품을 하고는,

"종혁이는 자나?"

뻔히 눈앞에 자고 있는 것을 보면서도 이렇게 물었다. 형수는 무엇이 그다지도 즐겁고 흐뭇한지 싱글벙글했다.

"네, 벌써 두어 시간 잤는데, 그냥 자는군요. 아까 낮에 기집애가 업구 나가더니 서너 시간 밖에서 잘 놀았어요. 노곤해졌나 부지."

"날씨가 이젠 차지는데 조심해요. 감기나 들지 않게."

"네."

형수는 공손하게 받았다.

다시 형님은 진수 쪽으로 돌아앉으며 은근하게 물었다.

"그래, 그 판문점이라나 하는 덴 어떻든?"

'굉장히 두텁군, 낯가죽이.'

진수는 그렇게 생각하며,

"네, 그저 뭐."

하고 또 우물쭈물하였다.

Jinsu responded with an awkward smile. "It was okay. It was worth seeing."

"What were they like?" Older Brother asked.

"Well, um…"

His voice trailed off. He didn't know what to say.

A condescending smile flicker across Older Brother's lips.

Here we go, the belittling smile for those beneath you that builds the wall of authority.

"Is my dress shirt back from the cleaners?" Older Brother already moved on and asked his wife.

"Yes. That little maid of ours said she had to wait there ten minutes or so. They were busy at the cleaners. She should have come back and gone back later. But no, she just had to sit around there doing nothing. Anyway, she brought it back," Sister-in-Law declared with a playful look at Jinsu.

"The director's going to the United States tomorrow. I'll have to see him off at the airport. What do you think? It would probably be best if you went too."

Sister-in-Law's face flushed. She must have been delighted at the opportunity to play such an important role.

"I wonder how long he'll be gone. His poor

일순 형수도 비로소 이 집 맏며느리답게 여유 있는 웃음을 웃으며 진수를 쳐다보았다.

"무섭지 않습디까? 우린, 생각만 해두 을씨년스럽기만 허지, 원."

"……"

진수는 할 말이 없어 대꾸를 않는데, 형수가 갑자기 문을 열며,

"얘얘, 순아."

하고 은근자중한 목소리로 부엌 쪽에다 대고 불렀다. 대답하는 기척이 없었으나 형수는 그냥 나직하게 말했다.

"상 채려 들여라아. 찌개 냄비는 대강 끓으면 내놓구, 할머니 상부터 어서 채려라."

부엌에서 그냥저냥 대답이 없자, 형수는 발끈했다.

"얘얘, 순아, 기집애가 귀가 처먹었나."

비로소 부엌에서 가느다란 목소리로 대답이 새어 나왔다.

"어서, 상 채려. 할머님 상부터 채리구, 동태 냄빈 내놓구."

시원시원히 소리를 지르고는 형님을 흘끗 쳐다보며 사뭇 상냥스러운 낯색이 되었다.

"저 동태찌갤 끓였거든요. 어머님이 어찌나 좋아하시는

wife—she can't stand being alone. I heard she had her diamond ring stolen just the other day. How could she let such a thing happen. True, she *is* kind of scatterbrained. What time is the flight? It's been a long time since I saw his wife. It will be good to see her."

Older Brother yawned and changed the subject again. "Is Jong-hyeok asleep?" he asked, even though he could see the baby sleeping right in front of him.

Sister-in-Law smiled broadly, as if there were cause for her to feel considerable pleasure and satisfaction. "Yes, for over two hours already. The maid took him outside earlier this afternoon and he must have played for three or four hours. I guess he's all done in."

"The weather's getting colder, so be careful he doesn't catch a cold."

"I'll be careful," Sister-in-Law replied in a deferential tone.

Older Brother turned back to Jinsu. "So what's this Panmunjom place like?" he asked quietly.

He's really something.

"Well, it's, you know," and he let his voice trail off again.

지……."

그러나 형님은 가타부타 대답이 없이 다시 진수를 보며 딴소리를 꺼냈다.

"진국이가 돈을 좀 부쳐 달란다지?"

"네에."

"얼마나 부치면 좋을까?"

또 이렇게 혼자소리 반, 진수에게 반, 뜨악하게 물었다.

"글쎄요."

마침 어머님이 들어오셨다. 그러자 형님은 덮어놓고 골치가 아픈 낯색부터 하였다.

형수는 자는 애의 머리를 조심스럽게 쓰다듬으며 앉음새를 바로하는 시늉을 했다.

"앤 자니?"

하고 어머니가 물었다.

"네에."

형수가 금세 꺼져 들어가는 목소리로 대답했다. 어머니는 흘낏흘낏 형님을 건너다보며 잠시 방 안의 분위기를 살피다가, 한참 만에야 진수 쪽으로 머리를 돌렸다.

"어딘가 갔다 온다더니 무사했니?"

"네."

The next moment Sister-in-Law was acting the oldest daughter-in-law of the house to perfection. "Weren't you frightened?" she asked Jinsu with a self-assured smile. "I mean, just thinking about it is so depressing."

Jinsu couldn't think of anything to say.

Sister-in-Law turned and opened the door. "Sun-a, Sun-a," she called out toward the kitchen in a dignified tone. There was no answer, but Sister-in-Law continued in a low voice, "Prepare the dinner tray and bring it in. Leave the stew to boil and bring in Mother's meal first."

There was still no reply from the kitchen.

"Sun-a, hey, are you deaf?" she called, her voice rising in anger.

The maid finally acknowledged her in a weak voice.

"Hurry up and bring in the tray. Mother's first— just leave the stew for now," Sister-in-Law snapped, turning toward Older Brother again and giving him an affectionate look. "I made some pollack stew. Mother's favorite."

Instead of acknowledging Sister-in-Law, Older Brother glanced at Jinsu. "I suppose you heard that Jinguk wants us to send him some money."

"그럼 무사하지, 무슨 일이 있겠어요. 어머닌 괜히 걱정이시어."

하고 형님이 괜스레 퉁명스럽게 말했다.

어머니는 조금 무안을 당하는 낯색으로 잠시 말이 없다가 진수에게 조심조심 또 물었다.

"또 쌈이나 안 나겠더냐? 난리 말이다, 난리."

"네."

형님이 오만상을 찡그리며,

"에이 참, 쓸데없는 챙견을 하서, 어머님은."

하고 신경질적으로 말하고는 휙 밖으로 나갔다. 어머니의 눈이 쓸쓸하게 형님의 그 뒷모습을 쳐다보았다.

"괜히들 그러는구나. 무슨 말을 원, 얼씬 못 하겠구나, 쯔쯔쯔."

형수는 얼굴이 홍당무가 되어 난감하고도 미안한 표정을 하며 더욱 머리를 수그리고 자는 애 머리를 쓰다듬었다.

열한 시가 지나서야 진수는 자리에 누웠다. 종일 버스 속에서 시달린 데다가 바싹 긴장을 했던 탓인가, 온몸이 노곤하였으나 정작 쉬이 잠은 오지 않았다.

폭이 넓은 푸른 강물이 급하게 흘러가고 푸른 옷을 입은 그녀가 노래를 부르면서 그 물에 떠내려가고 있었다.

"Yes, I did hear that."

"How much should we send?" he asked lackadaisically, half to himself, half to Jinsu.

"I'm not sure."

Mother came in. A pained look creased Older Brother's face, as if he had a headache.

Sister-in-Law carefully ran her fingers through the sleeping baby's hair and made a show of sitting up straight.

"Is the baby asleep?" asked Mother.

"Yes, he is," replied Sister-in-Law in a scarcely audible voice.

After several glances at Older Brother, Mother looked around the room as if sizing up the general mood. Presently she turned toward Jinsu.

"So you've been on a trip. Everything safe and sound?"

"Yes."

"Of course he's safe and sound. Why wouldn't he be? You're such a worrywart, Mother," complained Older Brother with unnecessary brusqueness.

Mother looked a bit put out and fell silent for a moment. "There's not going to be another war, is there? No more fighting, right?" she asked cautiously.

강둑에 선 그를 올려다보자 안타까운 표정으로 물속에서 손을 빼내어 흔들었다. 소곤대는 목소리로 급하게 조잘대었다.

들키지는 않았어요. 당신은 오른편으로 나가고 난 왼편으로 나가기를 잘 했어요. 나는 정말 와들와들 떨었지요. 그러나 그것이 바로 우리 현실이야요. 너무 통달한 체하지 마세요. 비가 지나가자 눈부시게 활짝 개었잖아요. 가을 햇빛이 정말 눈부시더군요. 빗물이 수증기가 되어 소리를 지르면서 올라가고, 그러나 하늘은 흠뻑 그것을 빨아들여 구름 한 점 없이 맑았었잖아요. 언제쯤 우리에게도 그렇게 사악 구름이 가실 때가 오려는지요. 당신은 지프차에서 나와선 시큰둥하게 우울한 낯색이시더군요. 막사에선 동료들이 한참을 찾았대나 봐요. 그 소린 날 뭉클하게 했어요. 난 거짓말을 했죠. 그냥 서 있던 자리에서 있었다구, 괜찮더라고. 그러자 그 땅딸막한 사람은 이렇게 말했어요. 김 동무는 역시 단단하거든 하고. 어쨌든 감사해요. 물큰물큰한 그 이역의 짙은 냄새에 잠시나마 홍건히 취할 수 있었어요. 난 원래 초행길이 아니야요. 단골이지요. 이를테면 당신 말대로, 졸음이 오는 듯한 그 남쪽 분위기, 기지개를 켜는 듯한 감미한 맛, 적당하게만 퇴폐

"No, there won't be," said Jinsu.

Older Brother scowled. "More useless worrying, Mother," he declared with annoyance, getting up abruptly and leaving the room.

Mother looked forlorn as she watched him make his exit. "There's no reason for him to act like that. You've got to be so careful what you say around here. The slightest thing..."

Sister-in-Law turned as red as a cherry. A perplexed, apologetic expression came over her face—she lowered her head even more and continued stroking the baby's hair.

It was after eleven when Jinsu went to bed. His nerves had been on edge all day. And he'd been tossed around on the bus. He was dead tired. But he had a hard time falling asleep.

The broad, blue expanse of a fast river. There she was, dressed in blue, singing as she floated downstream. She spotted him standing on the bank. She raised an arm from the water and waved, an earnest, anxious expression on her face. She began to speak rapidly in hushed tones.

"They didn't find out. You going out the ride side, me going out the left, that was smart. I was quaking like a leaf. That's the reality we face. Don't pretend

99

적인 것이 풍기는 그 완숙한 냄새, 조금쯤 무리를 해도 용서가 될 듯싶은 펑퍼짐한 언덕 같은 관용, 조금쯤 쓸쓸하고 괴괴한 분위기가 때에 따라서는 애교에 넘친 적당한 허풍, 당신들이 자유라고 일컫는 그 권태가 섞인 분위기는 확실히 짙은 냄새로 휩싸요. 반드시 악착같이 정연한 논리로 쓸모 있게 사느니보다, 여유 있게 자기를 누리는 맛, 누리는 것은 거드럭거리는 거지요. 곧 진력이 나고 권태가 오고, 그렇지만 사는 맛치고는 최고급일 거야요. 약간은 그렇게 살 만도 할 것 같긴 해요. 돋아 오르는 아침만 맛이 아니라 해가 기우는 저녁녘도 맛은 맛일 테지요. 야심에 찬 어린 치기(稚氣)도 치기지만, 길가의 늙수그레한 노인이 누리는 적당한 무위와 적당한 권태도 맛은 맛일 테지요. 그러나 그런 분위기도, 전 이미 익숙해 버리고 쉬이 졸업해 버리고 말았어요. 다만 판문점으로 오는 날은 기분이 좋아요. 무작정 냄새가 좋아요. 하지만 자기의 분수, 스스로 지녀야 할 태세를 추호도 잃지는 않아요. 남쪽에서 오신 풋내기 손님도 대뜸 알아볼 줄 알아요. 무척 순진하시네요, 제가 안내해 드릴게요, 이런 표정을 지을 줄도 알아요. 이러다가 혼쌀이 나게 걸렸었지요. 당신은 무서운 구석이 있어요. 물론 신사적이었고 피차 연민

you know everything. The sky was so clear after the rain, wasn't it? And the autumn sun was glorious. The rain turned to steam and raced back up to the sky. But the sky was able to absorb all the moisture, remaining spotlessly clear. Not a single new cloud appeared. The day will come when all the clouds disappear for us too. You looked so terribly depressed when you got out of the jeep. It turned out they'd been looking for me. I froze when I heard that. I lied, told them I'd stayed put where I had been before it started pouring, told them I was fine. Then the short guy spoke up for me. Said that Comrade Kim was really tough. Anyway, thank you. I was able to lose myself in that thick, heavy fog coming from a strange place. It wasn't my first time there, you know. I'm a regular by now. I was able to experience that sweet, comfortable feeling you said exists in the South, the feeling you get when you're dozing off, an appropriate decadence that has come into its own. A life such as that is like the gentle slope of a hill. You may go a little too far but you'll always be forgiven. There is sadness where you find such a life, a sense of solitude in the air. Empty words overflow with just the right amount of playfulness. You find there a life riddled with the ennui you call freedom, shrouded

으로 헤어지긴 했지만, 날 흔들어 놓으려구 해요. 어느 깊숙한 독(毒)의 도가니로 떨어뜨리려고 해요. 그런 건 못써요. 밝고 긍정적인 색채만 중요해요. 비록 지나치게 상식적이고 조악하다고 하더라도 차츰 성숙되게 마련이야요. 지금 중요한 건 거칠게 터전을 닦는 일이야요. 안녕, 빠이빠이. 불쌍해요. 당신이 불쌍해요. 착잡한 혼탁 속에서 주리를 틀고 계시지요. 그 범상한 속물적인 일상에 진력이 나셨지요? 지금 당신의 형님 방에선 바야흐로 사랑이 들끓고 있어요. 그런 것은 확실히 멋있을 거야요. 어디서나 멋있을 거야요. 이런 그리움을 그리워해 보았느냐고 물으셨죠. 우스워라. 사람들은 부끄러워서 그런 이야길 마음대로 못 해요. 그런 점은 어느 세상에서나 마찬가지지요. 너무 솔직해지는 것도 병이야요. 당신은 분명 그런 병이 있어요. 와작와작 자신을 깨물어 먹고 싶어 하는 병이. 당신이 불쌍해요. 빠이빠이. 우리, 어디서나 만나질까요. 어느 언덕에서나 만나질까요. 당신이 선 언덕에 해가 지고 있어요. 산그늘이 내려와요. 어머나아, 당신도 잠기시는군요. 안타까워라. 어둡기 전에 어서 돌아가세요. 문을 잠그고 그 쓸데없는 생각에 잠기세요. 기도를 드리세요. 유구한 생각에 잠기세요. 쓸모없는 당신의 그 사변에 마음

in layer upon layer of drowsiness. Taking the time to enjoy yourself, to explore who you are, is much more of a vainglorious enterprise than living purposefully in accordance with a strict, unyielding logic. It's not long, no doubt, before you're sick and tired of such a life, but still it probably offers the best you can get out of your time on earth. Such a life might even be worth living. The arrival of morning makes life pleasurable, but so does the setting sun of evening. Certainly we must treasure the untested youth full of ambition, but we must also value the old man sitting on the side of the street doing nothing, experiencing just the right amount of dreariness. But I'm already so very familiar with such a condition—I've long since moved beyond it. Anyway, I feel good on the days that I go to Panmunjom. The atmosphere is altogether agreeable. But never for an instant do I forget my position or the proper attitude I should take. I spot the first-time visitors from the South right away. I know how to behave toward them, how to tell them they seem so naive, how to show them around. But today my soul was shaken at its very core. You've got a scary side to you. Of course, you were very much the gentleman. And we were able to part on good terms, each with a sympathetic under-

껏 황홀하세요. 빠이빠이, 안녕. 내 이 혼자 감당해야 하는 비밀은 약간은 무게를 지녔어요. 이런 것 좋을까요? 그러나 안심하세요, 불원간 부숴넬 거야요. 안녕, 빠이빠이. 그녀는 쨍한 햇볕 밑을 급하게 흘러 내려갔다…….

이백 년쯤 뒤 판문점이란 고어로 '板門店'이 될 것이다 (비몽사몽간에 진수의 생각은 또 비약했다). 그때 백과사전에는 이렇게 쓰일 것이다. 1953년에 생겼다가 19××년에 없어졌다. 지금의 개성시의 남단 문화회관이 바로 그 자리다. 원래 점(店), 혹은 점포라는 말은 '상점'이라든가 '가게'라는 말과 동의어로 쓰였다. 이 어휘의 시초는 역사의 단계에 있어 초기 수공업 시대에까지 소급되어야 한다. 이미 고전경제학에 속하는 문제지만 자유기업이 성행하면서 이른바 소상인이 대두됨과 더불어 인류 역사의 각광을 받은 어휘이다. 그러나 이 판문점의 경우는 그런 전통적인 뜻의 점포가 아니라 희한한 점포였다. 이 점포의 특수한 성격을 밝히자면 당시의 세계정세, 그 당시 세계의 하늘을 뒤덮었던 냉전기류를 비롯하여 그 밖에도 6·25라는 동족상잔을 설명해야 하고, 그것은 적지 않게 거창하고도 구구한 일이기 때문에 여기서는 일단 생략하기로 한

standing of the other's position. But you did try to
shake me up. You tried to cast me into a vat of poi-
son. That wasn't right. What's important is to paint
the world in bright colors, emphasize the positive. It's
true we may be rough around the edges. But give us
time, we'll mature. For now the important thing is to
clear the field as best we can. So long, bye-bye. I feel
sorry for you. I do. You're caught, stretched out on
the rack. You live in a welter of confusion. You're
sick and tired of the dreary, mundane life enjoyed
by the philistines, aren't you? Right now, even as I
speak, it's getting hot and heavy in your brother's
room. It must be fantastic. A sea of delight. You
asked me if I'd ever hankered for that, remember?
Pretty funny. People are too embarrassed to answer
such questions. It's always been like that. Telling it
like it is can be a disease, you know, if you do it all
the time. And you've caught it, no doubt in my
mind. In the end, it will make you eat yourself alive.
I feel sorry for you. Bye-bye. Where will we meet
again? On top of a hill? The sun is setting behind the
hill where you're standing. The mountain shadows
are growing ever longer. Oh, my, it looks like they're
going to swallow you up. It's making me nervous.
Please, go home before it's too dark. Lock your door

다. 일언이 폐지하여, 회담 장소였다. 휴전 회담이라는 것을 비롯해서 군사정전 회담이라는 것이 무려 오백여 회에 걸쳐 있었다. '휴전 회담'이라든가 '군사정전 회담'이라는 말도 긴 설명이 필요한데, 여기서는 생략하기로 한다. 그 회담 기록이 적힌 거창한 문건이 지금 인류 역사의 기념비적인 익살로서 개성 박물관에 안치되어 있는 것은 이미 다 아는 사실이다.

얼마 전, 아프리카공화국에서 온 한 역사학자가 이 문건들을 전부 통독해낸 사실을 아는 사람은 다 알 것이다. 이것을 전부 통독해낸 것도 처음 있는 일이다. 그에게 문화공로훈장을 수여한 바 있지만, 그때에도 일부에서는 여론이 분분했다시피 약간 쓸개 빠진 짓이라는 느낌이었었다. 그러나 흑인종의 그 가상할 만한 끈질긴 정력과 참을성에는 누구나 감탄해 마지않았다. 이것을 통독해낸 그 흑인 박사의 결론은 이렇다. '이것은 걸작이다! 두말할 것도 없이 하여튼 걸작이다.' 일부에서는 이 결론이 야유 겸 스스로의 도로에 그친 노고에 대한 자위였을 거라고도 하고 있지만, 인간의 성실성이라는 것이 이렇게도 어이없는 데 소요될 수도 있다는 데 대한 경탄일 것이라고, 긍정적으로 해석하는 사람도 있는 것 같았다. 단도직입적으로

behind you and lose yourself in those useless thoughts of yours. Offer a prayer. Drown yourself forever in your thoughts. Forget yourself in the rapturous ecstasy of your fruitless meditations. So long, bye-bye. I feel weighed down by the secret I must carry. Could this be a good thing? But please don't worry. I'll get over it soon enough. So long, bye-bye."

And down the river she went beneath the scorching rays of the sun...

Jinsu's thoughts took advantage of his half-awake state to leap ahead of their own accord...

Two hundred years from now the term Panmunjom *will be an anachronism, the subject of an encyclopedia entry something along the lines of: "First appeared in 1953. Ceased to exist in 19XX. Formerly located in what is now the Cultural Center in the southern border of the city of Gaeseong. The* Jom *of* Panmunjom *literally means* shop *or* store. *One must look to the era when cottage industry first appeared in order to locate the first occurrence of the term* shop. *This transformation has, of course, been widely discussed in classical economics. As free enterprise began to flourish and small shopkeepers appeared for the first time, the term* shop *began to assume considerable historical significance. The case of*

얘기하자. 판문점은 분명 '板門店'이었고, 이 나라 북위 38도선상 근처에 있었던 해괴망측한 잡물이었다. 일테면 사람으로 치면 가슴패기에 난 부스럼 같은 거였다. 부스럼은 부스럼인데 별로 아프지 않은 부스럼이다. 아프지 않은 원인은 부스럼을 지닌 사람이 좀 덜됐다, 불감증이다, 어수룩하다는 데에 있다. 한데 그 부스럼은 그 사람으로서도 딱하게 알기는 아는 모양인데 어쩐단 도리가 없다. 그 부스럼을 지닌 사람은 그 부스럼을 모든 사람과 더불어 공동 책임을 지고 싶어 하고, 그 당대를 살펴보면 사실 그럴 만한 객관적인 내력도 어느 정도 있긴 있었다. 그러나 그 공동 책임이 도시 불가능했다. 그리하여 그 당자는 덜됐다고 해도 할 수 없고, 불감증이라고 해도 할 수 없고, 어수룩하다고 들어도 할 수 없게 되었다. 그냥 내버려 두기로 했다. 그럭저럭 세월이 지나는 동안 정작 당사자도 부스럼 여부는 까마득히 잊어버리고 멀쩡한 정상인의 행세를 시작했다. 어떻소, 이 부스럼, 신기하죠, 이쯤 내휘두르기도 했다. 제법 좀 사려 있답신 사람들이 구경을 오고 손가락질을 하면서 딱하게 여기는 얼굴을 하기도 하고 진단을 내리고 처방전을 만들어 책임의 소재를 규명하기도 했으나, 당자는 그저 웃어넘기거나 전혀 아랑곳하

Panmunjom *does not fit neatly into this paradigm. Panmunjom, that is, was a rather special kind of shop: it did not resemble a shop in the traditional sense. An elucidation of the singular character of this store requires an understanding of the contemporaneous geopolitical situation, beginning with the global significance of the Cold War and the fratricidal conflict known as the Korean War. The complexity of this history calls for an explanation beyond the scope of this entry.* Panmunjom *was a place where the two sides met to engage in negotiations. Ceasefire and armistice talks took place at* Panmunjom *on over five hundred occasions. The terms* cease-fire talks *and* armistice talks *similarly require explanations beyond the scope of this entry. Massive tomes containing the complete records of these talks are currently on display at the Gaeseong Museum. These records are widely considered one of the most monumental jokes in human history."*

"*The fact that a historian from a certain African republic recently has finished reading through each and every one of these records has drawn considerable media attention. He received a cultural achievement medal for becoming the first person to read these records in their entirety. There were those*

지도 않았다. 결국 사려 있답신 사람들도 그 선의의 사려를 팽개치곤 하였다. 왜냐하면 역시 자기 분수는 누구보다도 그 자신이 잘 알고 있다는 지극히 평범한 진실을 되씹게 마련이었다. 그리하여 그 부스럼은 날이 갈수록 더욱더 그 절체절명의 중량을 지니게 되어, 심지어 관광 유람지 구실까지 하였다. 판문점이란 이러한 세계 유일의 점포로서 문자 그대로 남북으로 난 두 개의 문이 판자문으로 되어 있어, 그 문을 열고 닫을 때마다 쾅 닫아도 한참을 흔들흔들했다. 천장이 낮은 길쭉한 단층집으로 휑하게 큼직한, 흡사 이 세기 전 국민학교 교실 같은 마루방인데, 신을 신은 채 드나들어도 괜찮게 되어 있었다. 문은 북문하고 남문이 있었다. 이를테면 그 문이 판자문이라는 말이다. 그런데 그 문을 두고 제법 근엄한(적당히 우울한 표정쯤 하고 맺은) 묵계가 있었다. 남문 사용자는 남문만 사용할 것, 북문 사용자는 북문만 사용할 것. 그리고 그 방 한가운데엔 가로줄이 쳐 있었고 그 줄을 사이에 두고 마주 무쇠 테이블이 놓여 있다. 각각 세 개씩 여섯 개의 테이블이었다.

그 테이블 뒤로 무쇠 의자와 작은 테이블과 또 다른 의자들과 마이크와 스피커가 우글우글 놓여 있다. 한 달에

who publicly called his efforts an utter waste of time, an exercise in futility. All, however, was unsparing in their praise of the energy and perseverance—both characteristic of the African people—that he brought to bear on the task. Upon completion of his labors, the African Ph.D. declared: 'It's a masterpiece! No other way to describe it—a masterpiece.' There were those who maintained that his conclusion pointed to a certain sarcasm combined with an attempt to console himself for his wasted efforts. Others, however, took a more positive view, asserting that he was marveling at the extent to which humankind could afford to invest time and energy in such an unbelievably preposterous project."

"Panmunjom was located in Korea near the 38th parallel. It could be considered a monstrous conglomeration of impure elements. In other words, if Korea is thought of as a person, Panmunjom was a boil located somewhere in the chest area. Not an especially painful boil, no doubt because the afflicted person was something of a simpleton, not quite up to par, somewhat numb in both mind and body. The person did seem aware of the extent of the misery associated with such a boil. Nevertheless, there didn't seem to be anything that could be done about it. The

한 두세 번 그 판자문이 사용된다. 열 시 가까이 되면 남쪽과 북쪽에서 각각 자동차와 버스가 굴러 온다. 살기가 등등해서들 서성댄다. 북문과 남문이 쿵쾅쿵쾅 열리면서 남문 사용자들과 북문 사용자들이 용건을 떠메고 우르르 들어선다. 후덕후덕들 자리를 차지해서 앉는다. 연필과 백지를 꺼내고 더러 저희끼리 귓속말을 주고받는다. 드디어 남문 사용자들의 거두가 들어선다. 훤칠하게 키가 큰 미국 사람이다. 남문으로 들어선 사람들이 일제히 일어서서 예를 표한다. 쇠붙이 의자의 마루에 부딪는 소리가 시끄럽다. 이어 북문 사용자의 거두가 들어선다. 역시 북문으로 들어온 사람들이 일제히 일어서서 예를 표한다. 드디어 양편이 다 자리가 잡히고 잠시 그럴듯한 침묵이 흐른다. 이렇게 되면 그 테이블 한가운데로 가로지른 흰 줄이 제법 경계선다운 육중함을 지니고 부각된다. 객관적인 당위성이 느껴지는 것이다. 이렇게 하여 소위 회담이 시작된다. 한국말과 미국말과 중국말이 교차된다.

판문점 근처에 이렇다 할 집이라고는 없고, 부속 건물들만이 몇 채 띄엄띄엄 서 있었다. 판문점 앞은 들판이었고 뒤는 펑퍼짐한 언덕이었다. 지금의 개성시 통문로 거리가 앞에 해당되고, 문화회관 벌판이 뒤편에 해당된다.

*person wanted everyone to share equal responsibility
for the occurrence of the boil. Indeed, an examina-
tion of the period under question reveals the existence of objective grounds in support of such a position. It proved impossible, however, to secure the
acceptance of others of any responsibility for what
had happened. There was nothing to be done. The
person was simply considered a little slow, a little
insensitive to pain, a little foolish. The person decid-
ed just to let things go. As time went by, the person
forgot that the boil had any effect on the body and
began to act as if everything was completely normal.
Indeed, the person even began to go around displaying the boil: 'What do you think? Isn't this boil quite
miraculous, a real curiosity?' People who considered
themselves thoughtful and cultured came to have a
look, pointing at it, sympathetic looks appearing on
their faces. They offered diagnoses, wrote out pre-
scriptions, suggested explanations as to what was
responsible for its occurrence. The person in question, however, would either laugh them off or pay
them no heed. Eventually, these purportedly well
intentioned, thoughtful people gave up trying to do
anything about the problem. They came to the com-
monsensical conclusion that in the end it was only*

이 얼마나 어이없는 일이었고 민족의 에너지를 쓸데없이 좀먹는 일이었던가. 통탄, 통탄이다. 우리의 조상들이 그 때 그 시절에 그 짓을 하고 있었다는 걸 상상해 보라. 더구나 외국 사람까지 주역으로 끌어들여서 말이다. 근엄하게 우울한 표정으로 그 문을 드나들었다는 것을 상상해 보라. 그것이 그때에는 상식으로 통했을는지 모르지만, 이런 놈의 상식이 어찌 통할 수가 있었더란 말인가. 바로 한가운데 가로지른 선이 지금 문화회관의 변소에 해당된다는 것이다. 고증학자 설 교수의 설에 의하면 변소 속의 변기가 바로 경계였다니 더구나 익살이 아닐 수 없다. 앞으로 문화회관에서 일을 보시는 분들은 쭈그리고 앉아 심심하거든 이 점을 한번 음미해 보시도록. 최근 설 교수의 그 설을 둘러싸고 분분한 논쟁이 있었던 사실을 아는 사람은 알 것이다. 그 선은 변소의 변기가 아니라 지금의 변소 문에 해당된다는 이설이 있었던 것이다. 이것은 참 유쾌한 논전이어서 우리들의 관심을 집중시킨 바 있었는데, 이 논전에서 우리는 우리 시대의 가상할 만한 큰 특징을 발견할 수 있었던 것이다. 2세기 전에는 이러한 종류의 논쟁이란 쓸개 빠진 어처구니없는 회화에 속했을 것이라는 사실이다. 인간 생활의 기본적인 여건이 해결되지 않았던

natural that the diseased person would know better than anyone else what to do."

"Years passed, and the boil expanded to a monstrous size. Things eventually reached the point where it became a tourist attraction. This place called Panmunjom became a shop like none other in the world. As the term Panmunjom, 'a shop with wooden doors,' implies, it indeed had two doors made of wood, one facing south, the other north. These doors would rattle in their frames every time they were opened or shut. The shop itself was a long, single-story building with a low ceiling. Inside, the spacious room with its wooden floor resembled an elementary school classroom of two hundred years ago. It was perfectly acceptable to enter and exit the building without removing one's shoes. Two doors— one to the South, the other to the North. Both made of wood. There was, moreover, a tacit understanding that one should assume a properly dignified, melancholic expression when entering the room through these doors. The southern door was reserved solely for the use of those from the South; likewise, the northern door was to be used only by those from the North. A line was drawn across the center of the room, dividing it in half. Six metal tables had been placed in the

조건하에서의 정신 상태의 양상을 이해하는 데 이것은 퍽 많은 것을 시사해 준다. 최근에 와서 문제가 되는 것은 여가의 이용과 자극의 발견, 경이의 창안이다. 최근에 와서 우리들의 취미가 굉장히 미세해지고 세분화된 사실을 새삼 상기해야 할 것이다.

다시 해가 뜨고 지고, 뜨고 지고, 서울은 이리저리 뒤채면서 들끓었다. 바야흐로 장면(張勉) 정부는 정국 안정의 사명을 짊어지고 가파른 언덕을 기어오르고 있었다. 신민당의 분열이 신문 지상에 클로즈업되고, 개각을 둘러싼 여론이 분분했다. 정부는 온 신경을 국회의 의원 분포에 소모했다. 정치자금의 염출로 민주당과 신민당의 실업계를 위요한 이면공작이 불을 뿜었다. 이 틈서리로 혁신계가 머리를 내밀었으나 그것도 벌써 이리저리 갈라졌다 붙었다 요동질을 할 뿐이었다.

진수는 취직 건 때문에 아침 일찍부터 돌아다녔다. 사흘쯤 희소식이다가도 닷새쯤 무소식이고, 이런 연속이었다. 이 다방 저 다방 들러 커피를 사고 혹은 얻어 마시고 매일 대여섯 잔씩이나 마셨다. 그 사이 어머니가 급하게 돌아가셔서 사나흘쯤 북새를 치렀다. 조카아이의 네 돌

center of the room, three on either side of the line."

"Metal chairs had been placed behind these tables. Several smaller tables, more chairs, and an array of microphones and loudspeakers had been placed farther back. The wooden doors were used two to three times a month. A little before ten o'clock in the morning cars and buses would pull in from both sides, North and South. Members of the opposing delegations would walk up and down in an agitated fashion, as if they were thirsting for blood. The northern and southern doors would bang open and the respective parties would stream into the room ready to tackle the issues at hand. They would bustle about settling themselves into their proper chairs. Then they would pull out their pencils and a few blank sheets of paper. Periodically one of them would lean over and whisper something to the person sitting next to him. Finally the leader of the delegation from the South would enter the room—an American of towering stature. The members of the South's delegation would all rise to pay their respects to him. The metal chairs grating against the floor of the room would create quite a din. Shortly thereafter the leader of the North's delegation would appear. The members of the North's delegation would follow

생일날에는 집에서 조촐한 파티가 있었다. 짝짝끼리 춤을 추기 전에 마루에 밀가루를 뿌리고 전축을 틀었다. 형수는 그 조금 큰 체대에 펑퍼짐한 한복 차림으로 형님의 어깨를 잡고 돌아갔고, 형님도 형님대로 어깨가 꾸부정해서 두 사람 다 삐딱한 모습으로 스텝을 밟았다. 미국으로 갔던 전무와 형수의 그 에스 언니도 초대되었다. 그들도 둘이 얼싸안고 춤을 추었다. 진수는 한구석에서 웬일인지 부끄럽고 쑥쓰럽고 자꾸 두 볼이 근질근질했다. 한순간 문득 전등이 꺼졌다. 동시에 전축도 멎었다. 마루에 치마 끌리는 소리와 잠시 수런거리는 소리가 일더니 소파에들 앉았다. 식모아이가 급하게 초를 켜 와 이 구석 저 구석에 세워 놓았다. 담소가 시작되었다.

"참 야단이야, 전기 사정이 이래 놓으니!"

누구인가가 이렇게 투덜거렸다. 형수는 주인으로서 제 책임이기나 한 것처럼 미안해 하였다. 부엌 쪽을 향해 한껏 우아한 목소리로,

"애야, 순아아, 초 몇 자루 더 켜오나아."

했다.

"하긴 전등불보다도 초를 켜는 것도 멋이야요. 분위기가 더 좋아요. 안온하구 쉬이 분위기가 익어요."

suit in rising to acknowledge his entrance. Finally the members of both delegations would take their seats. An appropriately long moment of silence would ensue. It was at this point that the white line dividing the tables would stand out in relief, taking on the gravity appropriate to a boundary line. The line would, at this moment, be invested with a sense of objective legitimacy. The preliminaries dispensed with, the meeting would officially commence. Three languages would be used—Korean, English, and Chinese."

"There were no houses worth mentioning to be found in the vicinity of Panmunjom, only a scattering of auxiliary buildings. Wide fields stretched out in front of the place, while behind was a gently sloping hill. The road presently leading to Gaeseong passes by what used to be the front of Panmunjom; the current annex to the Gaeseong Cultural Center is located behind the former Panmunjom. It bears mentioning how ludicrous the activities that took place there were, the extent to which the nation's energy was needlessly wasted. Lamentable, simply lamentable. One need only imagine our ancestors engaging in such behavior. To add insult to injury, they brought in a foreigner to play the lead role. Imagine the way

처녀인지 부인인지 분간이 안 가게 양장을 한 여인이
말했다.

"하긴 옛적 서양 귀족들은 초를 배치하는 것도 격조에
속했답디다. 그 집의 품격을 알려면 초의 배치 여하를 본
다더군요. 사모님께서도 한번 솜씨를 보이시지."
하고 그 옆에 앉았던 혈색 좋은 사내가 말했다.

"제가 원체 격조가 있어야죠. 막 굴러먹었는 걸."

형수가 이렇게 받고는 무엇이 우스운지 이상한 목소리
를 내며 짧게 웃었다. 다른 사람이 전혀 받아 웃지 않는
것을 알자, 약간 무안해 하며 필요 이상으로 침착한 표정
이다가,

"참, 김 전무님, 미국 가셨던 얘기나 하시지요."
하고 조심조심 말했다.

"……"

그 전무께선 덩치에 어울리지 않게 수줍은 표정을 하였
다. 순간 전무의 부인이 입을 실쭉하고는 이편을 얕잡아
보듯이 말했다.

"통 얘길 안 해요. 처음 갔을 때나 신기하지, 이젠 하도
가봐서 그저 그런가 봅디다."

"그렇겠죠."

in which they assumed those dignified, melancholic expressions as they passed through the doors. Perhaps at the time it all passed as ordinary behavior, but it is difficult for us today to see how this could have been considered a state of normalcy.

"The rest room of the Cultural Center now sits precisely on the place where the boundary line dividing the room in half was drawn. The whole matter becomes even more absurd when we recall that according to the eminent historian Professor Seol, it is the toilet that now sits upon the former border. In the future, perhaps those who find themselves bored as they sit upon this toilet can ponder the significance of this fact. We must note, however, that Professor Seol's theory remains controversial in the academic world. Some maintain that it is not the toilet that rests upon the former boundary line but the door to the toilet. In any event, it is a fascinating debate, one that certainly has drawn considerable attention."

"This debate, moreover, allows us to discern the nature of the age in which we live. Two hundred years ago such an argument would have been considered mindless, utterly preposterous. From this, in turn, we can gain considerable insight regarding the psy-

하고 형수가 받았다. 비로소 당사자인 그 전무가 말했다.

"더더구나 이번엔 일이 좀 바빴어요. 서구라파 쪽으로 나 갔으면 억지로라도 틈을 내어 재미를 보았겠지만, 미국은 이젠 하도 다녀와서 뭐 그리 심드렁하더군요. 하와 이에서 며칠 더 묵을까 했는데, 정작 이틀쯤 있으니까 또 조바심이 납디다. 역시 집이 제일 좋아요."

"언니를 너무 사랑하시니까 그렇죠."

좀 전의 양장한 여인이 받았다.

"아끼긴요, 기념품 하나두 안 사왔습디다."

전무의 부인은 또 실쭉해지면서 받았다.

"그야 믿는 사이니까 그렇지."

전무가 말하자,

"믿는 나무에 곰팡이 핀답니다, 흥."

하고 대번에 부인이 코웃음을 쳤다.

'저 작자 꿈쩍 못하는군. 영 형편없군.'

진수는 한구석에서 이렇게 생각했다.

사실 그 전무 부인의 어딘가 횡포에 가까운 신경질적인 몸짓과 말투는 자리의 분위기를 싸늘한 것으로, 힘든 것으로 만들고 있다. 그녀의 남편은 물론이려니와 모두가 그녀의 눈치를 조심스럽게 살피곤 했다. 열 시가 넘어 전

chological condition that prevails when basic human needs are not being met. Our society has reached a state in which an abundance of leisure time has led consumers to demand ever more personalized and diverse forms of entertainment. It is this that has brought about the recent reliance upon shock value and the increasing turn to the sensational."

The sun rose, the sun set. A few days passed. Seoul was swept up in a whirlwind of activity. The Jang Myeon government was working to ensure a measure of political stability, struggling like a mountain climber up an arduous stretch. The splintering of the New People's Party dominated the headlines. The media were busy offering differing opinions regarding the shake-up of the cabinet. The government was spending all its energy on attaining a majority in the National Assembly. The Democratic Party and the New People's Party were locked in a fierce struggle behind the scenes, each attempting to secure the greatest possible amount of financial support from the business world. In the midst of all this maneuvering, progressive forces managed to make an appearance. But they too split into competing groups, reduced to doing nothing more than

깃불이 들어오자, 촛불 밑에선 어지간히 익어 보이던 분위기였으나 다시 생소해졌다.

마침 전무 부인이 남편에게 짜증 섞어 말했다.

"여보, 이젠 갑시다."

"그래, 슬슬 돌아가 볼까."

전무라는 자가 이렇게 뭣인가 카무플라주하듯 어름어름 받았다. 모두 후덕후덕 일어나서 귀가 인사를 했다.

눈이 왔다.

눈에 묻힌 판문점은 장난감처럼 동그랗고 납작해 보였다. 휑한 언덕에 선명히 돋보였다.

진수는 그날도 광명통신 기자 이름을 빌려서 갔다.

그녀를 만나자 말했다.

"눈이 왔어요."

"네."

그녀는 어느 구석 여운이 담긴 웃음을 웃으며 한순 얼굴을 붉혔다.

"처음 만난 거나 마찬가지군요. 다시 힘들어졌군요."

진수가 말했다.

"……"

generating noise.

Jinsu was busy from early in the morning scrambling around town for leads. It went in cycles—he'd manage to come up with stories for about four days straight, and then there would be nothing for five days or so. He'd stop in one coffee shop after another, sometimes buying for someone else, sometimes getting treated. He'd drink half a dozen cups a day. In the midst of all of this hustle and bustle, Mother passed away without warning. Everything was in a state of turmoil for about four days.

An elegant party took place on Jong-hyeok's third birthday. Flour was spread on the floor. Everyone paired off in couples and began to dance to the music wafting from the record player. Sister-in-Law, her large frame enveloped in a flowing traditional outfit, spun around with her arms resting on Older Brother's shoulders. Older Brother leaned into her, and the two of them went swaying around the dance floor. The director, the one who had recently traveled on business to the United States, had come with his wife, Sister-in-Law's friend. They also embraced each other tightly as they danced. Jinsu sat in a corner and watched. For some reason he felt self-conscious and embarrassed—he could feel

그녀는 말없이 고개만 끄덕였다.

"그렇게 인정 같은 것에만 매달리지 마세요. 당신 주변에 있는 사람들이 헐벗고 있는 것을 생각하세요."

그녀는 또 그 투의 약간 준엄한 표정이 되며 말했다.

진수는 씽긋이 웃으며 말했다.

"천만에, 내 주변은 풍부해요. 도리어 너무 풍부하고 무거워서 탈이지요. 덕지덕지한 것이 참 많이 들끓고 있어요. 몇 겹으로 더께가 앉아 있지요. 도리어 헐벗은 것은 당신이지요. 당신은 새빨간 몸뚱이만 남았어요. 모두 털어 버리고 너무너무 알맹이 알몸뚱이만 남아 있어요."

그녀는 피이 하듯이 웃고 말했다.

"아주 벽창호군요."

저편엔 외국인 부부 기자가 여전히 가지런히 붙어 서 있었다. 남편은 역시 고불통을 물었으나 들이빠는 기척이 없고, 아내는 그 남편을 따뜻하게 정이 담긴 눈길로 건너다보고 있었다. 어느 안방에 단둘이 마주 앉아 있기나 한 것처럼.

안경잡이와 그 '누님'께서는 오늘은 다소곳하게 머리를 맞대고 정말 오랜만에 만난 오랍누이이기나 한 것처럼 수군대고 있었다. 스피커 소리가 왕왕 울렸다. 그녀는 남쪽

his cheeks getting hot.

Suddenly the power went out. The record player stopped. There was a momentary hubbub as dresses swished across the floor. Everyone sat down. The maid hurriedly brought in candles, placing them in the corners of the room. They all began to chat.

"What a mess. How could the electricity go out like this!" someone complained.

Playing the proper hostess, Sister-in-Law immediately took responsibility for the outage, expressing her apologies to everyone present.

"Sun-a, Sun-a, bring out a few more candles," she called out to the kitchen in a dignified and elegant voice.

"Actually, candlelight lends more atmosphere to a room than electric light. The ambiance is much more refined. Much more serene," declared a woman in Western clothes that made it difficult to tell whether she was married or single.

"Indeed, the Western aristocrats of long ago always considered the location of candles in the home indicative of one's cultural refinement. In other words, they would determine the level of a person's sophistication by taking note of where the candles in any given room had been placed. You

사람과 북쪽 사람이 여기서 만날 때 으레 짓는 그 경계와
방어 태세가 껴묻은 표정으로 피해서 갔다. 그 뒷모습을
건너다보면서 진수는 생각했다.

'기집애, 조만하면 쓸 만한데, 쓸 만해.'

혼자 쓸쓸하게 웃었다.

《사상계》(3월호), 1961

should take this opportunity to let your skills shine," proclaimed a healthy-looking man sitting next to the woman in Western dress.

"I don't have much in the way of sophistication. You can think of me as someone who came wandering in off the street," replied Sister-in-Law with an incongruous laugh, as if she found something terribly amusing about her remark. When no one else gave the slightest sign of joining in, she seemed deflated, an unnecessarily staid expression clouding her face.

"Oh, yes, Director Kim, how about telling us about your trip to America?" she asked slowly and carefully.

Director Kim assumed a bashful air, one that seemed out of kilter with his large, solid build. His wife produced a sour expression and cast a belittling glance his way. "He won't discuss it. The first time he went there, he was in awe of the place. But he's been there so often now that it doesn't seem like much anymore."

"I can see how that would happen," said Sister-in-Law.

Director Kim finally spoke up. "What's more, I was particularly busy this time. If I'd gone to Europe, I would have somehow found the time to do some sightseeing. But I've been to the United States so many times, it's lost its novelty. I thought I'd stay a few extra days in Hawaii, but I started getting antsy after only two days. I guess it's true, after all, that there's no place like home."

"It's because you love your wife so much," said the woman in Western attire.

"Far from it. He didn't even bother to bring me back a souvenir," complained Director Kim's wife with the same sour look.

"That's because we're so close there's no need for trifles like that," said Director Kim.

"Don't count on it," his wife snorted.

Jinsu remained sitting in a corner of the room. *He's completely under her thumb. No way he'll ever be able to make a move.*

Director Kim's wife did, in fact, exhibit a nervous streak, one that almost bordered on violence. Her words, the way she moved, seemed to put everyone on edge, casting a damper over everything. Not only her husband but everyone else as well kept a careful watch on her in an effort to anticipate her mood swings. The electricity came back on a little after ten, and the familiarity that had developed under the candlelight disappeared, replaced by a general awkwardness.

"Let's go, dear," said Director Kim's wife peevishly.

"Yes, I suppose we must be on our way," Director Kim hastened to respond, as if he was trying to cover something up.

The others in attendance jumped to their feet to bid them farewell.

It had snowed. And to Jinsu the snow made Panmumjom look like a collection of toys, the buildings standing in relief against the hill in the background.

Here he was again, reporting for the *Gwangmyeong News.*

"It snowed."

"Yes, it did," the woman replied with a suggestive smile, blushing.

"I guess it's the same as when we first met. It's not going to be easy this time either," said Jinsu.

She nodded, a severe expression returning to her face. "Don't be so sentimental. Think of all the people barely able to put clothes on their backs."

Jinsu laughed. "No, the people around me are living lives of splendor. The problem is that they're weighed down with too much luxury. Encrusted in layer upon layer of it. Actually, you're the one who barely has any clothes on your back. All that's left of you is your ruby-red body. Everything's been stripped off. All that's there is sheer nakedness."

"You really are pigheaded, aren't you?" She was unable to suppress a laugh.

The two foreign reporters were standing, as before, side by side across the way. The husband still kept his pipe in his mouth without smoking it, the wife still regarded him with warm affection. They looked as comfortable as if they were alone in their own living room.

Black Rims and his 'older sister' were quietly chatting. They looked like they really were brother and sister meeting after a long separation. The loudspeakers kept producing a twanging sound. The woman walked away. She wore a guarded, defensive expression, the look those from both South and North have whenever they meet each other at Panmunjom. Jinsu watched her leave.

Girl's not bad, not bad at all. I'd take her just as is.

He smiled bitterly.

Translated by Theodore Hughes

해설

Afterword

남북의 사이에서

이수형(문학평론가)

1961년 3월에 발표된 「판문점」이라는 소설을 이해하기 위해서는 무엇보다 먼저 '판문점'이라는 고유명사의 의미를 파악해야 한다. 소설의 한 대목에서 주인공 진수는 200년 뒤의 미래에 간행될 백과사전을 상상하면서 거기 쓰여 있을 내용을 다음과 같이 생각한다. "(판문점의) 특수한 성격을 밝히자면 당시의 세계정세, 그 당시 세계의 하늘을 뒤덮었던 냉전기류를 비롯하여 그 밖에도 6·25라는 동족상잔을 설명해야 하고, 그것은 적지 않게 거창하고도 구구한 일이기 때문에 여기서는 일단 생략하기로 한다. 일언이 폐지하여, 회담 장소였다. 휴전 회담이라는 것을 비롯해서 군사정전 회담이라는 것이 무려 오백여 회에 걸쳐

Between North and South

Lee Su-hyeong (literary critic)

In order to understand "Panmunjom," a short story published in March 1961, we have to understand, above all, the meaning of the proper noun "Panmunjom." At one point in the story, Jinsu, the main character, imagines an encyclopedia entry for this noun two hundred years in the future.

An elucidation of the singular character of this store requires an understanding of the contemporaneous geopolitical situation, beginning with the global significance of the Cold War and the fratricidal conflict known as the Korean War. The complexity of this history calls for an explanation

있었다."

1910년부터 시작된 일본의 식민치하로부터 1945년 해방된 한국은, 그러나 해방과 동시에 북위 38도선을 기준으로 미·소 양군의 분할 점령을 맞는다. 1950년, 해방 이후 현재에 이르기까지 한반도 최대의 사건으로 기록되고 있는 6·25(한국전쟁)가 발발했으며, 미국을 비롯한 16개국 군대로 구성된 UN군과 중공군이 남북한을 지원해 참전함으로써 국제전으로 비화된 전쟁이 교착 상태에 빠지자 1951년부터 휴전회담이 개시된다. 위의 설명에서도 알 수 있듯이, 판문점은 2년여에 걸친 장기간의 회담이 진행되고 휴전협정이 조인된 장소이다. 그뿐 아니라 지금까지도 분단된 상태인 남북한의 회담이 이루어지는 대표적인 장소이기도 하다. 한국인들에게 판문점은 6·25와 분단, 그리고 남북 대치의 상징으로 받아들여진다.

소설은 통신사 기자 신분을 빌려 판문점에서 열린 회담을 취재하러 간 진수가 거기서 북한의 여기자와 만나 나누는 대화가 주된 내용을 이루고 있다. 20대의 젊은 남녀 사이에 있을 수 있는 미묘한 분위기가 언뜻 비치는 가운데 진행되는 그 대화에서 진수는 사람이란 어떤 "효율의 데이터"로만 간주될 수 있는 존재가 아니며, 사람마다 지

beyond the scope of this entry. Panmunjom was a place where the two sides met to engage in negotiations. Cease-fire and armistice talks took place at Panmunjom on over five hundred occasions.

In 1945, Korea was divided at the 38th parallel and occupied by the US and the USSR at the same time as it was liberated from the Japanese colonial rule that had begun in 1910. The Korean War, the biggest incident in post-liberation Korea, broke out in 1950 and soon developed into a full-blown international war, as UN troops from sixteen countries, including the USA, and China participated in it as allies of South Korea and North Korea. When the war was at a stalemate in 1951, armistice talks began. As stated in the above quotation, Panmunjom is where two-year-long talks took place and the armistice agreement was signed. It is also where most talks between South and North Korea have been taking place until today. To Koreans, Panmunjom is the symbol of the Korean War, the division of the country, and the confrontation between South and North Korea.

The short story is mostly about conversations between Jinsu, a reporter from a South Korean

니고 있는 내면의 부피와 깊이는 한이 없다는 요지의 말을 건넨다. 이러한 진수의 생각은 혁명의 대의명분이 아무리 좋은 것이라 해도 그것이 인간의 욕망을 억지로 조율하거나 조절해서는 안 된다는 작가 자신의 생각을 반영한 것으로 볼 수 있다.

지금의 시점에서 보면 진수의 생각은 별로 위험하지도 않고 오히려 상식적인 것으로 받아들여질 수 있지만, 이 소설이 발표된 1960년대에는 남북한의 젊은이들이 만나 사적인 차원에서 분단과 정치에 대해 이야기한다는 설정은 민감한 문제를 야기할 소지가 다분했다. 이러한 점을 고려할 때, 「판문점」이 쓰여지고 발표될 수 있었던 자체가 극적인 변화를 겪었던 당시 한국의 정치 상황이 반영된 결과이다. 전쟁을 통해 강화된 반공주의를 등에 업고 비민주적이고 권위적인 통치를 행하던 자유당 정권은 1960년 봄 부정선거를 자행하다 국민의 저항에 부딪쳐 몰락한다. 사회 전반에 대한 민주화의 열망은 남북통일에 대한 요구로 이어지고 있었는데, 작가 이호철 자신의 회고에 의하면 「판문점」은 이러한 사회 분위기 속에서 그가 1960년 9월 실제로 판문점을 방문한 경험에 기초하고 있다. 말하자면, 「판문점」은 1960년 4·19(4월 혁명)가 없었다면 불

news agency who went to Panmunjom to cover one of these talks between the South and the North, and a female reporter from North Korea. In these conversations, in the somewhat suggestive atmosphere possible between a young man and a young woman, Jinsu expresses his thoughts that human beings cannot be considered simply "in terms of data to be made use of in the most efficient manner possible" and that individuals possess interior lives of infinite volume and depth. Jinsu's thoughts seem to reflect the author's own opinion that revolution, no matter how good its cause, should not dictate or control human desires.

From today's point of view, these thoughts of Jinsu's do not sound dangerous at all. On the contrary, they would be considered common sense. But in the 1960s, the very setting in which young people from South Korea and North Korea meet and have a private discussion about the division of the country and politics could have caused trouble for the author. This short story could be written and published only because the Korean political situation had just undergone a very dramatic change. The Syngman Rhee regime, which wielded undemocratic and autocratic power over the people, taking

가능했을 소설이다. 그런데 더 극적인 것은 이 소설이 발표되고 얼마 지나지 않은 1961년 5월, 쿠데타가 일어나 사회 분위기가 다시 한 번 급변했다는 사실이다. 「판문점」은 그 내용에서도 6·25와 남북분단 같은 한국현대사의 커다란 사건과 관련되지만, 그것이 발표될 수 있었던 것 자체가 4·19나 5·16 같은 또 다른 현대사의 흐름을 반영하고 있다.

advantage of their heightened anti-communist sentiment after the Korean War, had just collapsed after strong protest against election fraud in the spring of 1960. The ardent desire for democracy prevalent throughout society was also accompanied by people's strong demand for unification of the country. According to the author's own recollection, he wrote "Panmunjom" based on his own experience of visiting Panmunjom in September 1960 in this very atmosphere. In other words, "Panmunjom" is a story that would not have been written if the April 19th Revolution had not taken place. What is even more dramatic is that a military coup-d'état followed in May 1961, only a couple of months after this story was published, again radically changing the general social ethos. In its contents, "Panmunjom" reflects historical events of great significance in modern Korea like the Korean War and the division of the country. It also reflects, through the fact of its publication, another great historical movement that includes the April 19th Revolution and the May 16th Coup-d'état.

비평의 목소리

Critical Acclaim

생각건대 이호철 문학의 뼈대를 이루는 것이 분단과 실향이라고 흔히들 말하는 우리 시대의 민족사적 운명이라 한다면, 그 운명의 중압을 뚫고 하루하루 살아가는 선량하고 힘없는 소시민의 사소한 일상의 세부들이야말로 그의 문학의 살이다. 그러나 그의 문학적 성취를 단순한 세태소설로부터 구별하게 만드는 것은 일상성의 늪에 매몰되는 것을 끊임없이 방해하고 간섭하는 이와 같은 어떤 원천적 시선, 근본적 물음이 있기 때문이다.

염무웅

이호철의 소설적 출발은 전후 현실의 황폐성에 대한 인

In my opinion, while the national fate of our times, such as the division of the country and uprootedness, is the backbone of Yi Ho-chol's literature, trivial details of the everyday existence of good-hearted and powerless petty bourgeois trudging through their lives under the heavy burden of that fate are its flesh. But Yi Ho-chol's primary viewpoint and fundamental questioning continuously intervene and prevent these everyday details from being bogged down in mere mundaneness, and this sets his literary achievement apart from other simple fictions of manners.

Yeom Mu-ung

식과 이어진다. 동서 이데올로기의 냉전 논리에 의해 남
북으로 갈라선 민족이 한데 엉켜 싸워야 했던 6·25 전쟁
이 휴전으로 종식된 후에, 우리 민족에게 남은 것이라고
는 이데올로기에 대한 지독한 혐오뿐이다. 해방 직후 새
로운 민족국가의 건설을 꿈꾸었던 감격도 사라졌고, 새로
운 정치적 이념도 자취를 감춘다. 삶의 의욕마저 잃어버
린 세대들이 폐허 위에서 발견한 것은 그들이 어느새 상
실의 시대의 힘없는 주인공이 되어 버렸다는 엄청난 사실
이다. (……) 그러나 이호철은 여기서 주저앉지 않는다.
그는 이 황폐한 터전에 새로운 뿌리 내리기 작업에 관심
을 기울이게 되었던 것이다. 이른바 '소시민'이라고 명명
되었던, 그러나 사회학적 계층 개념으로 규정하기 힘든
사회적 부동세력 속에 자아를 던지고, 그는 위축된 개인
들의 틈에서 삶의 터전을 가꾼다.

권영민

이호철의 작품을 읽으면 특유의 입심이 이끌어 내는 현
실의 온갖 지저분한 잡동사니 면면들 저쪽에 그 악취와
독소들이 범접하지 못하는 맑은 기운이 서늘하게 드리워
져 있음을 느낄 수 있다. 그가 파행적인 우리 현대사의 한

Yi Ho-chol's stories begin with his keen sense of the devastation of postwar Korean reality. After the Korean War, in which a nation was divided by Cold War ideology and each side was pitted against the other, ended in armistice, the Korean people were only left with a strong disgust toward all ideologies. The strong desire for the founding of a nation state that people felt immediately after the liberation disappeared and new political ideologies held no meaning for them. The only thing generations that had lost even the will to live found in the ruins was that they were the powerless heroes and heroines of these times of loss... Yet Yi Ho-chol did not give up. He devoted himself to the task of supporting people's efforts to take root in this wasteland. He plunged into a sociologically amorphous floating social force called the "petty bourgeois" and cultivated his home among these shriveling individuals.

Kwon Yeong-min

While reading the works of Yi Ho-chol, we feel unblemished energy coolly surrounding them, an energy that can not be contaminated by the stenches and poisons emanating from all the sundries of our daily lives evoked by his characteristic volubili-

복판을 온통 상처 입은 채 살아오며, 오히려 그 같은 역사를 근본에서 비판하는 문학을 키워올 수 있었던 궁극적 요인은 이것이었다. 염무웅 교수의 "생각컨대 이런 일종의 생득적 순수성이 이호철의 작가적 생명력에 탕진되지 않은 싱싱함을 보장해 준 기초일 듯싶다"라는 지적은 이호철 문학의 핵심 하나를 찍어 올린 날카로움을 지닌 것이다. 작가 특유의 빠른 속도감의 문체 또한 이에서 비롯되는 것일 터이다.

정호웅

ty. It is thanks to this energy that he could create works fundamentally critical of the erratic course of our country's modern history, even while living, covered with wounds, in the midst of that history. Professor Yeom Mu-ung keenly observed one of the essential elements of Yi Ho-chol's literature when he said, "In my opinion, this kind of innate purity is the basis of the inexhaustible freshness and vitality of Yi Ho-chol's career as a writer." This energy of his is also the source of the fast pace characteristic of Yi Ho-chol's style.

Jeong Ho-ung

이호철

이호철은 1932년 3월 15일 함경남도 원산에서 2남 3녀 중 장남으로 출생했다. 중농 정도의 집안이었고, 조부 밑에서 천자문을 배우면서 비교적 유복한 생활을 하다 고등학교 3학년 때인 1950년 7월 인민군으로 동원되어 강원도로 내려왔고 그곳에서 포로로 잡혀 국군 헌병의 감시하에 북상하던 길에 자형의 도움으로 풀려나게 된다. 이호철은 부산으로 내려와 부두 하역 노동자, 제면소 직공 등을 전전하다가 미군정보기관 경비원 자리를 얻었고, 틈틈이 소설 습작을 했다. 1955년 《문학예술》에 「탈향(脫鄕)」을 발표하면서 등단한 이호철은 1962년 「판문점」으로 현대문학 신인상을, 1962년 「닳아지는 살들」로 동인문학상을 수상하는 등 활발한 작품 활동을 전개했다. 그럼에도 불구하고 작가로서 이름을 내는 것과 생활인으로서 사회에 뿌리를 내리는 것은 별개의 것이다. 고향과 부모형제를 떠나 단신 실향민으로 살아간다는 것, 존재의 근원으로부터 뿌리 뽑힌 삶을 살아간다는 것이 이호철의 소설에 있어 근본적인 규정성인 바, 남한에 정착하고 싶다는 욕망과

Yi Ho-chol

Yi Ho-chol was born into a family of middle-class farmers, the first son among five siblings—two sons and three daughters—in Wonsan, Hamgyongnam-do on March 15, 1932. Learning a primer of Chinese characters from his grandfather, he grew up in relatively affluent circumstances until he was conscripted into the (North) Korean People's Army in July 1950 when he was a high school senior. He was captured in Gangwon Province the same year and released thanks to his brother-in-law's intervention while being transferred as a prisoner of war guarded by the military police. Yi went to Busan and got a job as a watchman at the U.S. intelligence agency after working as a stevedore and as a laborer in a cotton-carding factory. Learning to write fiction in his spare time, Yi made his literary debut by publishing "Uprooted" in *Munhakyesul* in 1955. Actively pursuing his writing career, he won the 1961 *Hyundaemunhak* New Writer Award with "Panmunjom" and the 1962 Dong-in Literary Award with "Fleshes Being Worn Out." Nevertheless, to be

그 사회에 대한 비판적 태도 사이에서 고민하게 된다. 이러한 기로에서 이호철이 남한 사회의 소시민적 일상의 한계를 점검하고 그 한계를 넘어선 삶의 가능성을 모색할수 있었던 것은 세상을 읽는 해박한 지식과 삶에 대한 깊은 통찰력 때문이었다. 이호철은 청소년기에 김소월, 임화, 나쓰메 소세키를 비롯한 톨스토이, 고리키 등을 광범위하게 읽었는데, 특히 고리키를 위시한 19세기 러시아민중문학에 깊이 매료되었다. 또 공산치하에서 북한의 토지개혁 과정과 지방의 당조직 결성 과정을 목격하면서 이데올로기와 사람살이의 참뜻을 깊게 자각했던 것으로 보인다. 그래서 피난지 부산에 도착하기 전에 그는 이미 세계관이나 역사관이 웬만큼 틀이 잡혀 있었고, 전후 작가중에서 누구보다도 해박한 사회과학적 지식을 갖추고 있었다. 이호철이 긴 창작의 여정에서도 유신정권의 폭압에맞서 민주수호국민위원회 운영위원, 자유실천문인협의회대표를 맡는 등의 비판적 활동을 멈추지 않았던 것 역시이런 사정과 무관하지 않다. 분단 현실과 소시민의 일상에 대한 탐구를 지속해 왔던 이호철의 작품 세계는 자신이 살아온 과정을 소재로 활용하지만, 그렇다고 해서 단순한 개인사의 기록에 머무는 것이 아니라, 개인사를 통

established as a writer was one thing and to take root as a member of society was another. His works were fundamentally conditioned by the fact that he was living alone as someone uprooted from his home and family, from the source of his being. Therefore he was always wavering between his desire to settle down in South Korea and his critical attitude toward it. At these crossroads, Yi could examine the limitations of the everyday lives of ordinary people in South Korea and explore possible alternatives to these lives that would overcome such limitations, drawing upon his board knowledge of the world and his profound insights into life. During his youth Yi read widely: authors he read include Kim So-wol, Yim Hwa, Natsume Soseki, Tolstoy, and Gorky. He was especially fascinated by the nineteenth-century Russian people's literature spearheaded by Gorky. He seemed to have had an opportunity to think deeply about the true meanings of ideologies and human lives when he was observing the processes of land reform and local party organization in North Korea. Therefore he had already been more or less equipped with his own views on the world and history before he arrived in Busan. He was also armed with the most

해 민족사의 비극을 환기하고 궁극적으로 사회와 인간의
삶을 성찰하고자 한 끊임없는 노력의 결과이다.

extensive knowledge of the social sciences among postwar writers. It was no coincidence that Yi continued his critical activities, taking on the roles of a steering committee member of the National Committee for Safeguarding Democracy and president of the Writers Association for Practicing Freedom against the violent oppression of the *Yushin* regime. Yi's works are based on the biographical details of his own life in the process of his explorations of the everyday lives of ordinary people in his divided country, but they are not simple biographical records. They are the result of his endless efforts to evoke tragedies in national history through the medium of personal history and eventually to explore the natures and possibilities of human society and human lives.

번역 테오도르 휴즈 Translated by Theodore Hughes

컬럼비아 대학교 한국국제교류재단 한국학부 교수이다. 저서에 『냉전시기 남한의 문학과 영화:자유의 프런티어』가 있고, 『쥐불:일본제국 시기 한국단편선』을 공편했으며, 이호철의 『판문점:단편소설선』 등을 번역했다.

Theodore Hughes is Korea Foundation Associate Professor of Korean Studies in the Humanities at Columbia University. He is the author of *Literature and Film in Cold War South Korea: Freedom's Frontier*, the co-editor of *Rat Fire: Korean Stories from the Japanese Empire*, and the translator of *Panmunjom and Other Stories* by Yi Ho-chol.

감수 전승희 Edited by Jeon Seung-hee

서울대학교와 하버드대학교에서 영문학과 비교문학으로 박사 학위를 받았으며, 현재 하버드대학교 한국학 연구소의 연구원으로 재직하며 아시아 문예 계간지 《ASIA》 편집위원으로 활동 중이다. 현대 한국문학 및 세계문학을 다룬 논문을 다수 발표했으며, 바흐친의 『장편소설과 민중언어』, 제인 오스틴의 『오만과 편견』 등을 공역했다. 1988년 한국여성연구소의 창립과 《여성과 사회》의 창간에 참여했고, 2002년부터 보스턴 지역 피학대 여성을 위한 단체인 '트랜지션하우스' 운영에 참여해 왔다. 2006년 하버드대학교 한국학 연구소에서 '한국 현대사와 기억'을 주제로 한 워크숍을 주관했다.

Jeon Seung-hee is a member of the Editorial Board of ASIA, is a Fellow at the Korea Institute, Harvard University. She received a Ph.D. in English Literature from Seoul National University and a Ph.D. in Comparative Literature from Harvard University. She has presented and published numerous papers on modern Korean and world literature. She is also a co-translator of Mikhail Bakhtin's *Novel and the People's Culture* and Jane Austen's *Pride and Prejudice*. She is a founding member of the Korean Women's Studies Institute and of the biannual Women's Studies' journal *Women and Society* (1988), and she has been working at 'Transition House', the first and oldest shelter for battered women in New England. She organized a workshop entitled "The Politics of Memory in Modern Korea" at the Korea Institute, Harvard University, in 2006. She also served as an advising committee member for the Asia-Africa Literature Festival in 2007 and for the POSCO Asian Literature Forum in 2008.

바이링궐 에디션 한국 현대 소설 026

판문점

2013년 6월 10일 초판 1쇄 인쇄 | 2013년 6월 15일 초판 1쇄 발행

지은이 이호철 | 옮긴이 테오도르 휴즈 | 펴낸이 방재석
감수 전승희 | 기획 정은경, 전성태, 이경재
편집 정수인, 이은혜, 이윤정 | 관리 박신영 | 디자인 이춘희

펴낸곳 아시아 | 출판등록 2006년 1월 31일 제319-2006-4호
주소 서울특별시 동작구 흑석동 100-16
전화 02.821.5055 | 팩스 02.821.5057 | 홈페이지 www.bookasia.org
ISBN 978-89-94006-73-4 (set) | 978-89-94006-84-0 (04810)
값은 뒤표지에 있습니다.

Bi-lingual Edition Modern Korean Literature 026

Panmunjom

Written by Yi Ho-chol | Translated by Theodore Hughes
Published by Asia Publishers | 100-16 Heukseok-dong, Dongjak-gu, Seoul, Korea
Homepage Address www.bookasia.org | Tel. (822).821.5055 | Fax. (822).821.5057
First published in Korea by Asia Publishers 2013
ISBN 978-89-94006-73-4 (set) | 978-89-94006-84-0 (04810)